TRANS SAM

THE LEATHER JACKET

CHRIS PELZ

Pelz Productions!

CONTENTS

In Memory of
Wendy G.
She was the best of friends.

PROLOGUE

Hi, I'm Samantha, or Sam for short. I'm glad you're reading this book. I'm writing this to tell you my story and because we're in danger.

You're from the Eighth Realm. There are twelve realms that make up existence. There is an evil being named Lucien who is attempting to take over the twelve realms ... all of existence.

I'm going to tell my story as if it's happening currently, because that's how I feel like writing it. I need to tell you my story to explain myself and because I don't know what the future holds. Anyway, let's begin.

ONE

I LOOK in the mirror and frown. I don't like what I see. I'm 5 foot 2, with blue eyes and short black hair. I'm thin; I don't have much muscle on me, and honestly, I look a little wimpy. I have stubble on my chin, and I definitely look like a guy.

"Brian, the bus will be here soon!" The voice of my mother emanates from the bottom of the stairs.

God, I hate my life, I think. *At least I'm a senior in high school now. Not much longer 'til college.*

I go downstairs, rush outside and wait for the bus. I'm annoyed at the cold and that I still have to use the bus since I still don't have my driver's license.

"Today is the day, the day that I tell my friends I'm transgender," I say to myself. I remember when I was a lot younger and first learned the term. It was freeing knowing there was a word for what I am.

The bus pulls up and I get on. I pick one of the back seats and stare out the window.

I'm scared of how my friends will react. They're good, supportive friends, but I can't seem to shake the unease I feel.

I think back to when I was in fifth grade and about my friend Thomas. I was bullied regularly. One day someone pushed me into my locker and Thomas punched him, knocked him to the ground, jumped on top of him and punched him a couple more times. The kid was taken to the hospital with a concussion and Thomas was expelled. He had to move, and I lost my best friend.

I'm confident Thomas would have accepted me, and I assume my friends today will, but I'm still scared to tell them.

Before I know it, we're at school. I have four friends I feel like I can confide in: Rob, John, Travis and Jeremy. I decide I'll tell one at lunch and the other three after school when we play Dungeons and Dragons. The classes before lunch seem to drag on and I'm increasingly nervous.

I approach Jeremy at lunch. He's average height, with a muscular build and a mohawk haircut. He's white, like me and everybody else at my school.

He's a grade lower than I am, and Jeremy is the

exception to the rule that being on the football team makes you at least a little popular. I think he tries too hard. He copies what his teammates do in a fake, forced way.

We talk for a bit, then I tell him in a low voice so no one in the crowded lunchroom can hear, "I'm transgender." There's a long pause before he says, "Okay." There's another long pause. *Please*, I think, with a deep desire to be accepted.

"I've got to go to the library to work on homework," he says, clearly uncomfortable. He leaves, I feel horrible and reconsider telling my other friends.

———

Rob, John, Travis and I begin walking to Rob's house. A nice, gentle breeze moves past us.

These are my three closest friends, as usual walking so fast I have to jog to catch up when I repeatedly fall behind. This is my Dungeons & Dragons club.

We walk a block and turn left, headed into a straight stretch for the next 15 minutes. The houses we pass are decent but definitely not extravagant; our town is full of mostly middle-class people.

As we walk, I worry. Jeremy's behavior is the

main cause of my anxiety. *What if they have a negative reaction, too?* I think to myself.

I consider my life and friendship with each of them.

I could tell I was kind of different at an early age. I've always dealt with some dysphoria, not as much as a lot of people who are transgender, but it's been there. (You don't need to have dysphoria to be trans.) I did enjoy playing with boys' toys but wanted to play with dolls, too. There'd be times I'd enjoy wearing guy clothes and other times when I preferred girl clothes. One day, my cousin got some comics about a guy whose body changed to a woman's body because of water. I intensely wanted my body to change to that of a girl.

I was homeschooled until the fifth grade. Once a week I'd go to a thing called homeschool group, where a few families would teach together. That's where I met Thomas, the only kid my age. He was my first friend; he was my best and only friend at the time. We were inseparable.

Thomas and I went to public school together when fifth grade came around. I spent most of my first year being bullied. I was really socially awkward. I'd get nervous when talking to people I didn't know well. The anxiety of communicating and being around large groups of people could be crippling.

I was home-schooled again until seventh grade, when I went to a two-room schoolhouse. I made a couple of friends, but still wasn't used to interacting with a bunch of kids my own age.

When I got into high school, I went to a relatively small school compared to other high schools in the county, but it was dauntingly huge to me my freshman year.

I was still socially awkward (still am somewhat) and having a hard time adjusting. I only made two friends that year — Nick, who I would just joke around with at school, and John, a close friend now walking ahead of me.

I look at John. He's a little under 6 feet tall, has brown hair and is already losing a bit of it. He usually has a ponytail and always wears a hoodie — like he is now — unless it's ridiculously hot. I think back to how we met; I was overwhelmed and depressed at school one day, close to the beginning of freshmen year. He saw me outside eating lunch by myself and asked if I was doing okay. I said no; we talked for a while and found out we have a lot in common. We could easily make each other laugh. We became friends right away.

John and I hung out almost every weekend. We'd watch anime, movies and random TV shows. We'd also play video games and drink two liters of soda. Honestly, I probably would have committed suicide that year if I hadn't had him as a friend.

John is a bit nerdy, but even though he's about average build, he gives off a vibe of strength.

———

I look at Travis and think of our first extended interaction.

It's our sophomore year. The cloudless sky is full of stars, and I'm walking in the crisp late-autumn air on a sidewalk under a full moon. As I'm about to pass my high school, I see a figure leaning against one of its red brick walls. The figure is Travis.

He is cradling a guitar in his lap. He looks similar to how he looks now: tall, like 6 foot 2. He has short blond hair that is mostly covered by a beanie. He is extremely skinny, seemingly a little malnourished, in fact. I'd never tell him this, but he has feminine facial features that I envy. If not for his facial hair, he could pass as a tall woman if he wanted to and tried. Yeah, I'm a little jealous.

His shoes are off and he's enjoying the open air on his feet. He rests his guitar against the wall.

"Hey, Miller." He looks at me with his piercing green eyes.

"Hey, Travis." My mind registers he has a black

eye, a busted lower lip and some bruises on his left arm. "Are you okay?"

"Yeah. My stepdad won't be hurting me or my mom again." Travis stares at the moon.

"What happened?" I ask.

"I lost more and more fear of that man. Tonight, when he hit my mom, we fought. I sent him to the hospital," Travis says emotionlessly. "I don't know why I'm telling you this."

I sit next to him, leaning against the wall like he is. We talk for about an hour and a half straight.

———

I think Travis and his mom are really poor. When we play D&D after school at Rob's, we eat Pop-Tarts and drink Sunny D his dad buys; when Travis eats and drinks, he'll moan ever so slightly and I get the idea he kind of needs that meal.

Travis is the only one of us who is considered cool. This was not always the case, in fact, it's fairly recent. This year, he joined a band named "Beware the Dog."

Rob is wearing a ponytail like John. I think he's copying John in that respect. His hair is jet black, like mine. He, like the other two, are taller than me; he's about 5 foot 9. He has blue eyes. He's a little overweight, but not too much.

Like always, he's wearing black. Even though he wears the same all-black outfit every day, he's definitely not Goth. He's a minimalist. In his room there is a bed, dresser, television, video game console with a few games, some D&D stuff and two weeks' worth of the same outfit. Rob always says, "If it doesn't have utility and it doesn't make me happy, then there's no reason to have it."

We all look up to Rob a lot, though I think he kind of looks up to John. He's always the Dungeon Master in the game and is kind of our leader in real life.

John invited me to D&D sophomore year and I've been playing with them ever since.

Travis and I became friends soon after the night I just told you about, but it took a while to become friends with Rob. I kind of just tried to be his friend until he relented. Now Rob and I are really close; he's actually probably my best friend.

———

We get to Rob's house. As usual, we eat Pop-Tarts and drink Sunny D, then start playing D&D.

"I'm transgender!" I blurt out, a little too loudly while we're in the middle of playing the game.

There's silence for a moment.

Each of my friends has a different reaction. John

seems unfazed, Travis' mouth opens a bit in surprise and Rob's reaction is somewhere in between.

"Well, that makes sense," John says with a smile. "It's cool. Relax, you look so nervous."

"We're your friends, nothing will ever change that," Rob says, looking me in the eye.

Travis slaps me on the back lightly. "I'm glad you told us. We care about you. Wait, you identify as a woman, right?"

"Yes," I reply simply.

The guys ask a few questions and I feel relieved by their reactions. We go back to playing and before I know it, it's time to go home.

My dad picks me up and, in the car, says, "You seem happy."

"I am."

Tonight, I fall asleep with a smile on my face.

TWO

IT'S FRIDAY. I'm looking forward to the weekend.

Halfway through the day, I notice people acting weirdly around me, some even laughing for no apparent reason.

Rob rushes towards me. "Jeremy told everybody."

For a moment, I don't know what he means, then I feel raw fear.

"What do you mean?" I already know the answer.

"He told everyone you're transgender," Rob replies.

Like I said, our school is relatively small compared to other high schools in the county. Most of the school is like a long hallway with classrooms and lockers on both sides. It's small enough to assume that most if not everyone now knows.

It gets closer to the end of the school day. I'm walking between classes with my head down. I can tell people are looking at me more than usual. I don't make eye contact. Some act awkwardly around me, which makes me feel awkward.

Vanessa, one of my classmates, comes up to me with a smile.

"Is it true?"

"Yeah, I'm trans."

"Good for you! Be who you want to be." She smiles and continues to her class.

I have this same basic interaction multiple times. Each time, I feel happier and more confident.

———

I'm about to go home when a guy named Nate knocks into me, hard, almost knocking me over. "Queer," he says.

John is suddenly there, grabbing Nate by his shirt.

"Touch her again and I'll end you."

John looks at him with an intensity that scares Nate. After a moment, he pushes Nate away and Nate runs away.

My heartbeat increases and I start breathing heavily.

"Are you okay?" John asks.

"Yeah," I say anxiously.

John stays by my side while I calm down.

———

I miss the bus, so John drops me off at home.

I think about everything that happened today and I feel exhausted. I decide to take a nap. When I wake up, it's a couple of hours later. *Oh, I overslept*, I say under my breath.

Downstairs, my parents are already at the dinner table looking upset.

"We need to talk," my dad says.

My dad is muscular, tall, bald and tough looking, but he usually has a relaxed and calm demeanor. Not now. I can feel tension and a certain level of aggression. He's intimidating.

"Is it true?" my mom yells abruptly. She is a little shorter than me, has black hair and seems to always have a facial expression of displeasure.

"Is what true?" I ask, hoping it's not what I expect.

"Jeremy's mother called us," Dad says with a mixture of anger and disgust. "Did you tell everyone you're a girl?"

"No, Jeremy did." I feel horrible.

"Was he lying, or do you actually believe that?" Mom asks, livid.

"I am," I say, dread setting in. "I didn't tell you because I was scared you'd act like this."

I'm almost in tears.

"You're a disgrace to this family," Dad exclaims, with a frightening level of contempt.

The heavy atmosphere leaves me with a numb emptiness.

"Say you're sorry and say you're a boy," Mom demands.

"No, I'm a girl," I say in quiet defiance.

"Get out of my house!" Dad yells, slamming his fist on the table.

I look over at my mom and see that she looks like she wants to hit me. I rush out the door and leave the house I lived in for over seventeen years with tears streaming down my face. My parents are deeply religious, and I've always considered them good, loving people. This turn of events has left me devastated.

I wander the streets aimlessly as the temperature drops. I end up at the town's park. I sit down on a swing and glide back and forth for a while.

"What do we have here?" a voice exclaims behind me.

I quickly stop swinging, get up and turn around.

I see three guys who look to be in their twenties. All three of them are wearing light coats and jeans. They have short hair and are of average build. Two of them are tall and the other is noticeably shorter compared to them. The short one rushes forward, grabbing me.

"Help! Help me!" I yell in desperation before the guy covers my mouth with one of his hands. I have trouble breathing. I struggle, starting to panic.

I see a tall, fairly muscular figure punch one of the two guys who're not grabbing me in the side of the head. The punch knocks him unconscious, causing him to fall to the ground. The newcomer is black, wearing jeans, a green shirt and a leather jacket. He kind of looks like a badass. He punches the other guy in the nose; something snaps, he falls to the ground holding his face, then gets up and runs away.

The newcomer, who seems to be trying to save me, yells, "Let him go!"

The guy grabbing me tightens his grip for a moment, then lets me go and runs away.

My rescuer contemplates chasing the guy who grabbed me, but he cares more about my well-being. "Are you okay? he asks.

"No." I start crying.

My rescuer looks very concerned. "Are you hurt?"

"No. I'll be fine."

"Hi, I'm Thomas," he says, obviously still worried about how I'm doing.

"Thomas, Thomas Hill? Is that you? I ask, stunned.

"Yeah, Brian Miller. It's been a while," he says with a big smile.

I'm surprised we didn't recognize each other right away. It was probably because of the high-stress situation and the fact we weren't expecting to be reunited.

He looks over at a bench. "Want to sit?"

"Yeah," I reply, and we both sit on the bench.

I start to shiver, so Thomas puts his leather jacket over me. I feel safe.

"So why are you out so late by yourself?" He sits back a bit.

"My parents kicked me out of their house, and they disowned me," I say, stopping myself from crying more.

"Why? You don't have to tell me if I'm being too personal," Thomas says.

I pause for a moment. But I feel comfortable with him, so I tell him in a soft voice, "Because I'm transgender." I put my head in my hands "I knew they'd be upset, but I wasn't expecting this."

I feel a deep sadness.

He pauses for a moment then says, "Getting

kicked out, it's not your fault. You know that, right? Your parents just suck."

We sit as snowflakes begin to fall.

I look around. "Remember, we used to play in this park all the time."

"Yeah, we used to swing in those swings," he says, looking to his left.

He looks to his right at the rest of the play area, with a smile. "I really missed you."

"I missed you too." I say, hugging him.

THREE

THOMAS TAKES me back to his place, an apartment within walking distance of the park. It turns out he was taking a night walk when he saw I needed help.

We walk into his apartment. He gives me a quick tour. It's a decent-sized one-bedroom apartment. The apartment is very clean, like ridiculously clean. I can tell everything is in a deliberate place.

"Wow, your apartment's really clean," I say the obvious. "Your bed is even made; I never do that."

"I'm a little OCD," he replies.

We go into the living room, sit and talk for a couple hours.

"You're welcome to stay here as long as you'd like," Thomas says, lying on the couch. "I'll take the couch; you can crash on my bed."

I go to bed. The bed smells musky and nice like

Thomas. I fall asleep feeling drastically better than before Thomas showed up in my life again.

The morning seems to comes abruptly.

Thomas is already up. He shaves, does twenty pushups, some squats and stomach crunches, then makes us breakfast burritos. While he's making the food, I see inside his fridge. Like his apartment, it's very clean and there seems to be a specific order to it.

We talk for a while, then Thomas says, "I've got to go to work."

Thomas is a cook at a bar/restaurant. He's only a year older than me so he can't be a bartender, not that he wants to be. He leaves and I watch TV, not sure what else to do since it's Saturday and my homework is at my parents' place.

Thomas gets home late, and we have a late dinner of chicken, cut-up fruit and some vegetables. He seems really healthy.

"I forgot to tell you, you can have any of the food here," Thomas says.

We talk for a while about our lives since fifth grade. It turns out he'd been living with his grandma most of the time since he moved away, and moved back after he graduated high school last year. He wants to be a master chef someday.

Thomas cleans a little bit, does twenty pushups and we go to bed. Sunday comes quickly.

———

Sunday starts like the day before. After we finish breakfast, I give him a big smile knowing that he doesn't have to work today. We spend the day together, going on a long walk and just watching TV together. We binge watch a show called Art.I? where amateur and professional artists compete against art created by artificial intelligence. The art critics who judge the art guess which ones were created by people and which ones were created by A.I.

When it gets time to go to bed, I get anxious about school the next day. The whole school now knows I'm trans. I remind myself that my friends will be there to support me. It takes a while to fall asleep, but I do.

FOUR

I GO TO SCHOOL AND, for the most part, it's a normal day. Close to the end of the day, the principal calls me into his office. He looks to be in his fifties, is overweight, bald and always seems to be sweating regardless of the temperature.

"Your parents called me," the principal says. "What's your living situation?"

"I'm staying with a friend," I reply.

"Since you're almost eighteen, we're going to stay out of your business unless you need help." The principal looks concerned. "Do you?"

"No, I'll be fine," I reply, looking at the door. Even though he's being kind, I have a strong desire to leave the room.

"I wish you well. Let me know if you need help," he says, opening the door.

"Thank you, I will." I stand and leave.

———

I hang out with Rob and the guys. We play video games and I inform them what's going on. They are encouraging.

———

I go back to Thomas' place; I do homework and we hang out after he gets back from work. He lets me know that changes in routine are difficult for him, and I'm supportive.

———

Days go by and I pick a new name. Samantha, or Sam for short. As time passes, Thomas and I become closer and closer.

Rob and the guys — along with Thomas — are validating and start calling me Sam right away.

———

Before I know it, it's my birthday. Thomas and I go out to eat and then we go for a walk.

"I know things have been tough on you,"

Thomas says while we're walking. He stops and so do I.

"I really care about you." Thomas starts to fidget a bit.

"I really care about you, too," I reply. "Are you okay?" I ask, seeing that he's really nervous about something.

He looks at me anxiously for a moment, looking very vulnerable. "Can I kiss you?"

I'm surprised almost to the point of being in shock. After a moment I say, "Yes."

He leans forward and kisses me.

I stiffen up for a couple of seconds as my perception of our relationship significantly changes. It takes just a couple seconds for my body and mind to adjust to this new reality. The moment passes, and I relax and kiss back.

Thomas is my first kiss. I'm glad it's with my oldest and closest friend.

He holds me close. "You're my girl," he says in a soft voice.

We continue our walk holding hands. He repeatedly kisses the back of my hand randomly, with his eyes closed. It's all I can do to stop myself from dancing with joy.

———

The days seem to pass quickly. Thomas and I randomly message jokes back and forth, making each other laugh. I always feel comfortable with him. We completely understand each other.

Each morning, I wake up to a rose on the pillow next to me. I promise myself that I won't ever take him for granted.

I start dressing androgynously. I get bullied a little, but no one takes it too far; they know that if they did, they'd have to mess with Rob and the guys. Also, Thomas has picked me up from school often enough that people know about him, and they know there's a chance they'd have to deal with him as well.

Time flies and final exams almost catch me off-guard. I get decent grades but with graduation soon, I still don't know if I'll go to college or not.

———

Graduation is a little annoying since they won't use my preferred name. I wasn't really expecting them to, though, so it doesn't bug me too much.

———

We have a senior overnighter where we go on a bus and do stuff until the next morning. We go to a movie, then on a lake cruise that lasts a couple of hours, then finally to an old-timey western tourist trap where we dance and walk around town. The whole experience is pleasant, no one is mean and I have time to say goodbye to everyone.

I plan to only stay in contact with Rob and the guys and a couple of other people.

———

The summer starts out great. Thomas and I hang out when he's not at work and I'm not hanging out with Rob and the guys.

A little over half the summer passes as Thomas and I become closer and closer.

I think about him and our relationship. I can tell him anything. I feel completely comfortable when I'm with him. He's the first person I can 100% let my guard down with.

———

Around the end of summer, we talk a little about marriage, but plan on being together for a couple of years first.

I get a job at a gas station within walking distance of the apartment. I plan on saving up for a year for college.

I'm truly happy. Things are great, until one day in late fall.

FIVE

I WAKE up stretching with a yawn. I look over at the pillow next to me and raise an eyebrow.

There's no rose on the pillow, which is out of the ordinary. This is the first time that's happened since Thomas and I kissed. My eyes go wide and my heartbeat shoots through the roof when I remember I went to sleep before Thomas came home.

I get out of bed quickly, falling to the floor. I get up and frantically search the apartment. Seeing that he's nowhere to be found, I stand motionless in the kitchen, one of my hands on the side of my head.

A moment goes by and I try to calm down. An idea occurs to me. I call Thomas and get his voice mail. "Thomas' phone, you know what to do."

A bead of sweat runs down my face, falling to the ground as I call Thomas' work.

"Hello, this David, the Alibi is closed today." A tired voice answers.

"Hi, this is Sam. Is Thomas there?" I ask.

"Thomas ... Thomas was shot. He passed away late last night." It sounds like David is crying. "I'm sorry. He was protecting me ..."

I hang up and drop my phone.

I'm breathing heavily. I close my eyes, inhaling slowly through my nose, then exhaling with my mouth. I do this several times, calming myself.

"I can't handle this," I think to myself.

I begin cleaning the apartment, unconsciously trying to distract myself from this new reality. I make sure everything has order, structure. It feels like a ritual, like I can sense his presence beside me.

While cleaning I find a notebook. I open it and find it has only one page filled out. I read.

My Samantha
We meet once again.
I see her and look into her eyes.
The eyes that tear through the barriers, the walls I hide behind.
The eyes that can see through my masks,
through my facades, to see my naked soul.
She sees my guarded heart, melting my will,
making me vulnerable.

She whispers the unspoken words and asks the impossible.

I think, 'Do I know you?' seeing something familiar in those eyes.

I see her smile as the past collides with the present.

And we're left in a familiar place
Both warm and exciting.

We stand together in an unfamiliar place
we stand under the moon and the stars
unable to grasp such a vastness
we look at each other, content for the moment
tomorrow may contain trials and sorrow
but not tonight, not right now
we see the moonlight and know the moon
the stars, the sky are for everyone
but seeing the light reflected off the lake
that reflection we know is just for us.
Yes, we stand in this unfamiliar place
A place both scary and beautiful
terrifying and unexpected.

Samantha and I hold hands
as we walk.
I see the trees and the bark
while she sees the forest and the leaves.
While we walk, I see the branches and
she sees through them to the blue sky.

As the crisp wind passes us
it moves her hair and I look into her eyes
Her unbelievably blue eyes.
She doesn't need the makeup.
She doesn't need the fancy clothes.
She doesn't need the things she believes she
does.
She is beautiful just the way she is.
I wish she could see herself through my eyes.
Even with the trials and hardships in life that
can narrow my vision.
No form of evil, pain, cruelty in this world can
overshadow her beauty to me.
The way she smiles and shivers at the
same time
as snowflakes cover her hair and melt on her
face.
Her caring heart, her gentle soul, her loving
stare, the peace I believed was a lie
I realize that with her I'm whole.
That I need her in my life
Nothing has been clearer.
I know I will never make her as happy as she
makes me
As content
But that doesn't mean I'm not going to try
I will never stop trying
For her

She calms my restless mind.

When I'm with her there are times when I can
stop constantly thinking and just be

She's my girlfriend, my princess, my partner,
and best friend.

She's my love,

She's my soul mate.

I stop cleaning. I start to feel like I need some fresh air. I take a walk.

I'm really lucky to have had him in my life; he had the kindest heart.

Strangely enough, I start to think of the mundane things: the walks we took, us cooking together, listening to music, content just to be with each other.

I go to the park, sit on a swing and memories of our time together from childhood until the last time I saw him yesterday go through my mind. I look next to me at the empty swing, wishing with everything in me that he'd be there with me. The reality of his death fully sets in. I wail as tears run down my face.

A moment later I put my head down, my hands covering my face and muffling the sound of my sobbing. I feel lost.

———

The next couple of days go by in a daze. Thomas' family plans a funeral, and I go to it. His parents weren't happy with our relationship, but that seems not to matter now. They are very nice.

At the funeral, David comes up to me and says, "I worked with Thomas. He talked about you a lot, even more than he talked about cooking. It was obvious he really loved you. He'd want you to have this." He gives me Thomas' leather jacket.

"Tell me more about how he died," I say, seeking understanding and peace.

David looks at the ground like he's ashamed. "Thomas and I were outside. It was dark. A guy attacked me. Thomas fought him off and he ran. The guy must have come back with a gun, because someone shot Thomas several times from the shadows."

When I get back home, I put on the jacket and cry myself to sleep.

———

When I wake up the next morning, I feel strange. I stumble out of bed feeling taller. I walk into the bathroom and jump from surprise. The image that is looking back at me is a woman 6 feet tall with long, reddish hair. I look around and it takes a minute to realize it's me.

I look back at my reflection and gasp. "OH MY GOD!"

I continue staring at the mirror in shock. After some time, I look in my pants to see that I don't have a penis or testicles anymore. I take off my PJ bottoms and look at my new vulva. I touch my body all over, making sure everything is real.

I decide I want to see my full body. I take off Thomas' jacket and suddenly my body changes back to normal. I yell loudly; changing back freaks me out almost as much as the initial transformation.

I stand in front of the mirror, wondering if I just hallucinated the whole thing. After some time passes, I go back into the bedroom and start getting dressed.

"That was weird," I say out loud. I finish getting dressed, finally putting on Thomas' leather jacket. Right when I get the jacket on, the strange feeling occurs once again and I can tell I've gotten taller. I look down, my pants have become too short, riding up my legs. Luckily I'm wearing a baggy shirt. I grab my chest and feel breasts.

I go into the bathroom to see that my body has changed into the woman's body, the same woman's body as before.

I do an experiment, taking off the jacket, and I

change back into my normal body. I put it back on again and change into the woman's body. I take off the jacket and put it on multiple times. Each time taking it off causes me to change to my normal body and putting it on causes my body to change into the same woman's body. I finally leave it off, unsure how to process this. On the one hand, it's kind of awesome, but on the other hand I'm seriously scared that I might be having a psychotic break.

I suddenly realize it's time for work.

"Dammit!" I yell. When I couldn't get the day off after the funeral, I'd almost quit my job. I hide Thomas' (my) jacket, getting a little paranoid. Then I leave to go to work.

I have a hard time concentrating, thinking of Thomas and the jacket.

I almost forget, but I visit the landlord and take over the lease for the apartment.

When I get back to my apartment, I try my jacket on several times to check if it still changes my body. It does.

I call Rob and the guys and ask them if they can come over tomorrow. This surprises them, because they've never been to the apartment. They all say yes.

The next day I check again if the jacket still changes my body, and it does. I question my sanity.

Travis shows up first, then Rob and then John.

They sit down in the living room, and I look at them nervously as I grab my jacket.

"I have something to show you."

I put on my jacket, and I transform. All of them are in shock.

"What the fuck?" Travis says after a while.

"Is that you, Sam?" Rob asks, not quite believing his eyes.

"Yeah, I don't know what to make of this," I reply. "When I put on Thomas' jacket this happens, and when I take it off, I change back."

I take off the jacket and unsurprisingly turn back to the way I looked before.

"Does it do that to anybody?" John asks.

"I don't know," I answer, not having thought of that.

"Can I try it on?" Travis asks, curious to find out.

I think about it for a moment.

"Sure."

He tries it on, and nothing happens. Rob and John try it on after asking and they don't transform, either.

I try it on just to make sure it hasn't lost its mojo, and I transform.

"How does it feel when you transform like that?" John asks.

"My whole body feels really warm except my groin, which feels cold," I reply. "My privates changing kind of feels like a combination of how it feels when you're in really cold water and getting kicked in the crotch. It's actually not unpleasant, the only bad part is my chest hurts a bit as it's happening, but it's really quick."

"I don't know how to respond to this situation," Travis says. "What do we do now?"

"We could take a walk," Rob suggests.

We take a walk that loops around the elementary, middle and high schools. We talk about Thomas and everything going on in our lives. We decide to go to the local pizza place.

Rob asks, "Are you going to wear your jacket regularly?"

I think about it for a minute. "I'm not sure."

We get to the pizza place, eat and then I go back to my apartment.

————

Tonight, I lie on my bed and see that Thomas' mom called me. When I call her back, she tells me they saved $10,000 for Thomas' education and they want to give it to me. I say, "I'm not sure if I can accept that."

She insists and tells me I'm going to get the money this week.

———

Getting the money doesn't change my plans too much. I continue working at the gas station and sign up for fall classes at a community college when it gets close to summer.

It feels really weird getting money as a result of Thomas dying. But I think Thomas would be happy knowing I'm using a portion of it for education.

I don't wear my jacket much outside because summer is close and it's hotter. Also, surprisingly enough, even though no one would guess I'm a trans woman because I pass really well, I still feel some fear being seen in public in my woman's body. I feel freer when I'm in the jacket and just feel more like myself. It feels right but it's hard to explain. I know once I get used to being transformed in public, once I get over the initial fear, it will be great. So, I decide I'll start wearing it frequently in the fall.

I quit my job at the beginning of summer, learn to drive and get my license and a cheap car.

I pick Rob up for a drive. He gets in and is a little sweaty.

"Hey, Sam," Rob says, opening the car door. "I like your car."

My car is 19 years old. Too old to do anything music-wise with my phone or mp3 player. Old enough I could play a cassette tape if I really wanted to, but new enough to play a CD. It's a green four door, with a pretty well-kept interior.

We ride listening to the news on the radio for a while. They talk about some stuff I can't remember, and about new laws for the school systems in a couple of places. They change the topic and Rob turns off the radio. Rob knows a lot about what they were talking about. He tells me about how schools in a few states have effectively made it so teachers and students K-12 can't talk about any LGBTQ stuff, ever. If a kid has two moms or two dads, they're not allowed to acknowledge it or even that it's something that can happen. Gay teachers can't have a picture of their spouse on their desks. Textbooks — or any schoolbook, including books in the school library — can't contain any mentions of people in the LGBTQ community. Universities can lose funding if they don't do basically the same thing and books are being banned in public libraries.

I'm surprised he knows more about this than I do. *I need to pay more attention to what's going on in the world*, I think to myself.

"They want you dead," Rob says with a serious tone.

"What?" I respond. My heart rate increases as my mind grapples with what Rob just said.

"They want you dead," he repeats himself. "A

large percentage of people, including lawmakers, want trans people dead."

Rob sees I'm distressed by this and tries to cheer me up, largely because he wants me to feel better but also because the news is affecting my driving a little.

He talks for a while, then says, "Remember when John, Travis, Kenny, Nick, you and I got kicked out of the school library for playing Scrabble too loud?"

I give him a smile and feel a little better.

"Yeah, and then we went to the cafeteria and got kicked out of there, too, for playing Scrabble too loud. And then we went to the gym and were like, what happens if we get kicked out of here? Then lunch period was done."

We listen to music and just drive.

———

The summer days drag on. Each day I commit to a routine similar to the one Thomas had, the structure bringing order to the chaos in my life.

———

I move to the city that my college is in by the end of summer. The drive from my new apartment to Rob's isn't that far so I'll still be able to hang out with him, Travis and John frequently.

I start classes as it becomes fall. I picked general education classes, but I'm not sure what career path I want to follow.

———

One night I go for a walk. The sky is black. The air becomes chilly. I briefly consider going back to my apartment to get my jacket, but actually the cool air feels oddly nice.

The two streetlights in front of me are the only sources of light. Suddenly shadows are cast in the dim glow on the cement and on the wall of a building to my right.

Several figures suddenly move towards me.

"Out pretty late, aren't we?" one of them says with a chuckle.

I freeze and they surround me. One of them punches me in the face. I fall to my knees clutching my bloody face. I put my hands on the ground and launch myself forward to run away, but I'm pushed back to the ground. I'm on my hands and knees when one of them kicks me in the side and I crumble into the fetal position while gasping for air. An all-encompassing feeling of powerlessness consumes me as I black out.

I wake up hours later still on the sidewalk. I get up on wobbly legs. I disregard the idea of going to the hospital, since I can't afford any medical bills right now. I walk back to my apartment and go in. I walk into the bathroom holding back tears.

"Why would anyone do that for no reason?" I say to myself. I look at myself and see dried blood coating my face. I wince as pain in my side becomes intense.

I take off my shirt, then the rest of my clothes. There are bruises all over my chest and stomach. I take a shower. Warm water hits my face and washes the blood off me. I put my right hand on the wall, shifting my weight. I feel the water hit my body; the soothing warm water helps calm me down even though it hurts as it hits my wounds.

I finish the shower, dry off and put on pajamas. I become curious, I put on my jacket and transform. I'm surprised to find I don't look hurt; I look exactly how I usually look when I'm transformed. I also don't feel any pain or discomfort.

"What the hell?" I exclaim, perplexed.

At this point I start to feel tired, so I go to bed.

The next morning I wake up and brush my teeth. I'm curious once again. I take off my jacket to find I've transformed back to normal, looking like I never got beat up. I take off my shirt to confirm that yes, I'm completely healed.

———

One day when I don't have any classes, I decide to wear my jacket outside and interact with people while being able to pass as a woman. I go to a café and sit drinking coffee.

The café is fairly small, having three booths, one table and a little area to make coffee behind a counter. I find the smells of the establishment intoxicating.

A masked man comes in brandishing a gun. He's average height and a little on the skinny side. Even with the mask and weapon he seems anxious, scared, even. He yells for the owner to put the money from the cash register in a bag he's holding in his other hand. The owner does.

The robber looks at me and the other two customers in the café. He yells at an elderly man to give him his wallet. The man does, looking scared. The robber goes to the other patron, a lady who looks to be in her thirties who also looks terrified. He grabs her purse, putting it in the bag. He yells at her to give him her wedding ring. She tries, but it won't come off her finger. The thief becomes more and more agitated.

Suddenly, I get an overwhelming feeling that he's going to shoot the woman. I spring into action, crossing the café swiftly. The robber turns his head

at the sound of me leaving my seat. No sooner does
he turn his head than I knock his gun out of his
hand, then punch him in the stomach. He falls to
the ground, clutching his midsection.

I kick the gun away from the robber, pick it up
and give it to the owner of the café. I feel
compelled to leave. I dash out of the door and
begin running. I notice I'm running fast, seemingly
inhumanly fast.

I run to my apartment, go in and sit down. I
notice I'm almost breathing normally. I think about
what happened over and over, letting it sink in.

I call Rob and tell him what happened during
my last night walk and what happened afterwards. I
also tell him what happened at the café.

"I'm coming over," he says.

Rob gets to my apartment, and I let him in.

"I think you might be a superhero," Rob says
right away.

"What?" I reply, feeling like he's being
ridiculous.

"I think you might be a superhero," Rob repeats
himself. "Does your school have a gym?"

"Yeah, why?" I say, filled with strong curiosity. I
can see he has a plan.

"Let's go there," Rob says, seeming a little
excited.

We go to my school's gym, and I pay to use it

because I'm wearing my jacket and I don't look like I do in my school ID.

Nobody is using the gym, which is perfect for what Rob has in mind.

"What are we doing here?" I ask.

"We're testing your abilities," Rob replies.

We first go to the treadmill and I start using it. Rob turns it to the max and I run for 30 minutes without breaking a sweat or getting out of breath. Rob stops the treadmill and I get off.

"Take off your jacket," Rob says.

I do and transform like I always do. I try the treadmill again but. I get tired fast and can only do it for a short period of time before I have to stop.

"Damn, I'm pretty out of shape without my jacket," I say, out of breath.

"We probably should have had you use the treadmill without your jacket first, but it seems like you're in very good shape with your jacket on, and normal — if not less than normal — without it," Rob says. "Now let's see if you have super speed."

I put on my jacket and transform. We go to a basketball court, and I run around it as fast as I can. It impresses Rob and he says, "You have super speed."

We go to the weights, and he has me take off my jacket again. I transform and do some bench pressing and Rob spots me. We test my limits and

I'm embarrassed —it's likely that the majority of people could bench press more than I can.

I then put on my jacket and start to bench press weights. We put more weights on the bar and I keep doing it until we get to a weight amount normal for an amateur bodybuilder. After I succeed at bench pressing that, Rob says "We should stop. It's not safe because I'm not that strong of a spotter. Anyway I think you have super strength."

"Do you have a computer lab?" Rob asks, changing the subject.

"Yeah," I respond. I take him to the computer lab.

"Let's test if you have super smarts," Rob says, going on a computer.

He has me do a bunch of IQ tests with and without my jacket. Each test shows average or about average, which is my normal IQ.

"Well, I guess the jacket doesn't affect your intelligence," Rob says, sounding a little disappointed.

We go back to my apartment, and we test if I can read minds. I can't.

Rob goes to the other side of the apartment and says, "Try and hear what I whisper."

"You can't play as a bard in our group," Rob whispers and I can tell what he said clearly.

"You can't play as a bard in our group," I say with a smile, before he can ask me what he said.

"Super hearing!" Rob yells, raising his fists in the air.

Using spices brings us to the conclusion that my sense of smell might have been enhanced.

Rob calms down after a moment and says, "Try and shoot laser beams from your eyes."

I try and can't. I then try and look through one of my walls and some random items but am unable to.

"Let's take a break," Rob says.

We take a walk. By now, it's dark out.

"I don't know what I want to do with my life," I confess to Rob. "John's going to be a mechanic, Travis has his band, and you're working at the hardware store. Even superheroes in the comics generally work for a living. I don't want to work a dead-end job. What are your plans for the future?"

"I just plan to work at the hardware store, hopefully become a manager at some point," Rob begins. "You got to find your own meaning of life. One of the most beautiful things about existing is we get to choose our own. I get mine from the connections with the people I love."

"Sometimes I feel really lost," I admit.

"I think that's completely normal," Rob responds. "I never told anybody this, but I feel like the weight of the world is on my shoulders, like everything bad that happens is on me, like I let it happen. Even though I have very limited ability to control big-picture problems, I feel responsible. I think it's a type of arrogance."

"Well, you're definitely not arrogant," I assure him.

We walk for a while in silence.

"When parents tell their kids they can do anything they put your mind to, obviously they're lying," Rob says. "You're smart and kind-hearted. Everybody has limitations, but I don't know what yours are. Just believe in yourself, believe in yourself like I do."

We continue walking aimlessly down streets talking about what's going on in our lives and just random things when suddenly, we come upon a couple being robbed by five men.

I spring into action, rushing behind one of the thieves. I hit him on the back of the head, knocking him out. The other four turn their attention to me and away from the couple. The couple runs away.

One of the men rushes towards me. I punch him in the gut and he crumbles to the ground. I rush forward, punching one of them in the face, causing him to fall to the ground clutching his face. One of the two still standing lunges at me. He grabs me, trying to immobilize me. I kick the side of his leg causing one of his kneecaps to pop out. He falls to the ground, yelling in pain.

The last standing robber looks at the other four on the ground, then runs away.

"Who the hell are you?" the man who was punched in the gut yells.

Rob goes up to him, kicking his head and knocking him unconscious.

"She's a fucking superhero."

SIX

Two weeks go by uneventfully. Then one day I see a horrific story on the news: A little girl was shot and killed in a drive-by shooting.

My apartment is in an interesting spot. If you go left from my place you head into a bad part of the city; right is mostly peaceful. The murder of the girl is in the crime-ridden part.

I think long and hard and come up with a plan. I wait until dark. I put on my jacket and head left.

I know there are two prominent gangs in the city, the High Kings and the Valkyrie. I go into the High Kings' territory. The air is humid and there's light rain. The smell of gasoline from an unknown source fills my nostrils. It's chilly and I'm glad to be wearing my jacket for multiple reasons. I only see a few people randomly for a while; it's not a safe place to be out at night. I finally come upon what looks to be a drug deal. Two people standing under a lamppost near an alley exchange money for a small bag. I don't see the person who took the bag very well and he leaves. The guy who took the cash is wearing a brown coat, a beanie and, oddly enough, dress pants. He checks his phone.

I go up to the one who took the money and say, "Hi."

"You looking to buy?" he replies.

"I'm looking for the head of the High Kings," I say.

He looks at me with a mixture of confusion and, surprisingly enough, concern.

"You don't want to be mixed up with him. And it's dangerous to be out here alone."

I take out a hundred-dollar bill from my pocket and give it to him. He looks conflicted for a moment, then gives me directions to the gang's base of operations, which is where he expects Garcia — the gang's leader — to be.

I start towards the gang's base, my destination.

"Be careful," he says.

"Pretty nice drug dealer," I say to myself.

I make it to the base without incident. There seems to be a party. The building is two stories high with what sounds like a large group of people inside. Two men block the front door.

I think of a simple plan. I walk up to the men and say, "I'm here for Garcia."

They look at me, then each other. They pat me down, checking for weapons and I get the feeling they're mostly doing it just to touch me. They let me in. I get the sense they wouldn't have let me in if I looked like a guy.

I walk in and move through a crowd of people dancing to loud music. It smells like sweat, sex and bad decisions. Even though it's crowded, I get the feeling of loneliness.

I continue further inside. It gets progressively more cramped, and I feel a bit claustrophobic.

I see a few people doing drugs and a bunch of people drinking. I ask a random guy and ask for Garcia. He says he's not sure where he is.

I go up to multiple people and ask if they know where Garcia is. One of them leads me to a set of stairs. We go up to a wide area where I see a few people sitting on a long couch watching TV in front of a table with drugs on it. Nearby is a man sitting behind a computer desk counting money.

"Hey boss, someone here to see you," the man who brought me upstairs says.

The man behind the desk gets up and looks at me up and down.

"Can I help you?" he says with a grin.

"Your gang murdered a little girl a few days ago," I say, matter-of-factly.

"Yeah, and the men who did it are in jail now," the gang leader says with a frown.

"I have a proposition," I reply. "A new way to settle your disputes. Each week — or month — one member of your gang and one member from their gang have a fist fight."

Garcia thinks for a moment, then says, "Get lost."

"Aren't you sick of needless bloodshed?" I ask in desperation. "You need to stop the pointless violence."

"*I* need to ..." he begins, with a cold expression. "Leave or I'll need to break your kneecaps."

The guy who brought me upstairs leads me back down. On the way back home, it fully hits me how stupid and naïve I was being.

I'll have to figure out another way ... I think to myself.

———

The next day, I join a martial arts class. I continue with school during the day and at night, I patrol the streets.

I decide to fight crime. I ignore drug deals and general sex-worker transactions, as I'm a libertarian on social issues. I wear a black cloth mask, stop thieves and people being assaulted. I also stop the sex trafficking of some young ladies.

Most of the general public doesn't know about me, but rumors spread and I'm starting to make a name for myself. I think that — other than the people I'm fighting with — I have a good reputation. I continue my work as a vigilante into the summer.

I do well on my fall exams, and I do even better on my spring exams.

———

One summer night, though, things change. I walk right into a trap. I walk down a street in the shadows and see what appears to be a woman being assaulted. I rush to save her, and the woman and the guy who seems to be assaulting her stop. Both of them smile.

I'm surrounded by a large group of men who all look similar in the bad lighting. Several attack me. I punch the first one, knocking him out, and then kick several others to the ground. The group starts closing in on me. I try to fight my way out. I hear a loud crack of a metal pipe hitting the back of my head. The world spins, and I drop to one knee trying to stay conscious. I almost black out. Someone pushes me to the ground and some of the group starts kicking me.

I see a figure appear, attacking the men around me. He's fast and I'm not sure if he's moving so fast that he's blurry or if he is blurry because I'm almost unconscious.

Then I really do black out.

————

I wake up in my bed. I jolt upright and I'm hit with a searing headache and confusion. After a moment I quickly pat my chest and shoulders. I realize I'm not wearing my jacket.

I get out of bed, searching frantically for my jacket. I know in my normal body I'd lose in almost any fight. I can't find my jacket in my bedroom, so I leave the room and am confronted by a man wearing jeans and a T-shirt. He is a little taller than me in this form and he's a bit overweight. He's muscular. He's wearing a flannel shirt, dress pants and suspenders. He's kind of handsome. He has a stern look on his face.

"Hello, I'm Gideon," he says.

He sees I'm alarmed.

"I'm the one who saved you."

"Thanks."

I'm still concerned by the situation.

"How did you know where I live?"

"My master Rime told me." He pauses. "There's much I must tell you."

"Where's my jacket?" I ask, still not completely trusting my uninvited guest.

"In your coat closet. I took it off you on the off-chance you would attack me," he responds.

I go to my closet, get my jacket and put it on. "So, what do you need to tell me?"

"May we sit?" he asks, motioning to the living room.

My apartment is similar to the one Thomas and I had in size and layout, just not very clean. I go to my living room couch and sit. He grabs a chair from the dining room table.

"My master has chosen you to be a soldier in a war as old as time," he begins. "There are twelve realms that make up all of existence. Think of them as alternate universes. It's our duty to protect the realms."

I feel overwhelmed. I breathe in slowly and deeply, then exhale, calming myself. "This all sounds crazy," I say incredulously.

"As crazy as a jacket that changes your body the way that one does?" He gestures to my jacket.

"What do you know about my jacket?" I ask, thinking he has answers for me.

"Master Rime cast a powerful spell on it," he says.

"Why did he do that?" I ask.

"He originally chose your boyfriend to be one of the Chosen. Before he was murdered, Master Rime looked into his mind and learned of you," he says.

"So, he's like a wizard?" I ask.

"He's a powerful being," he replies, obviously annoyed.

"Was it the guy who attacked David who killed my boyfriend?" I ask right after the question crosses my mind.

"We think it was one of Lucien's men," he says.

"Who's Lucien?"

Gideon gets intense. "He's the right-hand man of the worst evil you can imagine."

"This is ... a lot," I say aloud. *I don't know if I can handle this. I wish Thomas was here*, I think to myself and sigh. "What else do you need to tell me?"

"You are from the Seventh Realm. You are needed. Not many people have the soul required to be one of the Chosen." He stands up. "I'll give you time to think."

"Wait, are you from this realm?" I ask.

"I'm from the Eighth Realm. The Seventh and Eighth Realms are unique because they are parallel universes and are very, very similar."

"When will I see you again?" I ask.

"When you are ready," he says before leaving.

————

I call Rob and tell him everything that happened. He is concerned and a little upset at me. He ignores the craziness Gideon told me and scolds me for not being more careful with the crime fighting. Then he seems upset with himself and says he wishes he could help more.

"Can we hang out this weekend?" he asks.

"Sure," I reply.

"See you then, have a good night," he says before hanging up the phone.

————

I wake up and it's Friday. I turn on the TV and eat a breakfast bar while watching the news. There's a story of humanoid animals being spotted around the city. *Yeah, right, probably a prank*, I think.

I spend the day on the internet searching for Gideon, twelve realms of existence and the Chosen. I don't find anything of value.

————

The next day, I meet up with Rob at the mall. Not a lot of people are around. We get something to eat at the food court and go shopping, mostly window shopping. Rob buys a new wallet.

"I'm really glad some malls still exist," Rob says, looking around.

Suddenly, we hear people yelling. A humanoid wolf rushes by people who are running straight towards me. He's a little under 7 feet tall, black fur over most of his body and a black nose. He seems powerful. He stops squarely in front of us.

"We must go. I am a soldier of the Third Realm. The barrier between our realms opened briefly. I need your help. Your government is after me and my kind," he says with urgency.

He seems in great pain for a moment, then transforms into a normal-looking guy a bit under 6 feet tall. He has shaggy black hair on his head and is in general pretty hairy, and he looks exhausted. "Please help," he implores me with a calm but urgent gaze.

I get a feeling, not completely unlike the feeling I had in the coffee shop when I knew the robber was going to shoot that woman. I have the feeling I can trust this person.

"We're taking him back to my apartment," I say, looking over at Rob. We lead him to my car, he gets in the back and we get in the front. We leave Rob's car at the mall, and I begin to drive to my apartment.

Rob looks backwards for a moment, then says in a low voice, "I hope we're making the right choice."

"What?" My reply seems barely audible over the pounding in my chest.

"Nothing," Rob responds.

Our new guest falls asleep and changes back to his wolf-person form.

When we get to my place, we are unable to wake him. He is very heavy, and I can tell under normal circumstances I wouldn't be able to carry him, but I have my jacket on and my extra strength makes it easy enough. We take him into my living room and lay him on my couch.

"Are you sure this is a good idea?" Rob asks.

"No, I'm not," I respond.

Rob and I wait till the wolf-man wakes up. It takes several hours.

"Ah, my head," he winces.

"What's your name?" I ask after a moment to let him fully wake up.

"Buusta," he responds. "I can tell you are one of the Chosen, but I don't know your name. What is it?"

"Sam," I reply. "This is Rob."

"So, there's a rift between your realm and ours?" Rob asks.

"There was a rift briefly," Buusta begins. "Lucien is experimenting. I'm not sure of his plans, but I know he will need to move his army between the realms if he wants to take over all of them."

"How many people got through the rift?" I ask.

"About a dozen," Buusta says. "Most are good folk." Then he says, "I'm starving."

I don't have much food in my apartment, so I don't know what to do for a moment.

"If you can transform back to looking human and stay that way, we can go out to eat." I say, evaluating the situation.

Buusta gets up and transforms.

I look at his muscular body and get a bit flustered. He's only wearing a pair of blue jeans. "I kept some of Thomas' clothes. Just a minute." I go into my bedroom closet and get sneakers and a shirt Thomas got for eating a five-pound burrito on one of our dates.

Buusta puts on the clothes. We have to cut the front part of the shoes open because his feet are a little bigger than Thomas'. The shirt is tight and rides up, showing Buusta's belly button. Buusta tenses up in pain. "It hurts when I change form and takes energy away from me."

We talk for a while, then decide to go to our favorite deli.

. . .

As we're heading home after our meal, something crashes into my car, causing it to almost flip over.

I look out and see a humanoid reptile. He's muscular, average height for a man and has green scales. His head is a cross between a crocodile and a human.

I see a building catch on fire out of the corner of my eye and a female-humanoid fox who is sending flames from her palms. The fox looks over at me and winks. Her slender form has red and white fur. She has big ears, black eyes, a large bushy tail and prominent teeth.

"I got the green one," Buusta says, getting out of the car.

I get out, too, and run towards the fox-person. She sends fire at me, and I'm hit with wave after wave of blistering heat. I feel immense pain as I reach my adversary. I kick at her midsection and connect. The fox doubles back, and we begin punching each other. I kick her in the chest, and she crashes to the ground. I lunge at her, and she sends a large blue fireball at me. I yell in pain as I pass through the fire.

I land on the fox, grappling with her and getting my arm around her neck. We struggle on the ground and, without thinking, I pull with all my strength. Her neck snaps.

I rise from the ground, gritting my teeth. The fire

burned away a lot of my clothes, but for some reason left my jacket unharmed. I have a little trouble breathing and smell what I think is sulfur. I go into the burning building and help a couple of people escape.

I see a few flashes in the distance, but it barely registers in my mind. I go to find Rob and Buusta.

Buusta thrusts forward at the lizard-man, bashing him in the side of the head. The lizard-man recoils, then leaps towards Buusta, striking him in the stomach. Buusta growls. The lizard-man hits Buusta in the ribs.

Buusta falls to the ground. The lizard-man laughs, right before getting hit by my car. Rob is driving.

The lizard-man hits the windshield and rolls over the top of the car. Rob is showered with shards of glass.

Buusta gets up and goes to his enemy. He jumps on top of him and starts punching his head, each time with increasing force. When his enemy's head caves in, Buusta growls.

I get to Rob and Buusta. Rob is obviously a little shaken.

"You ... you guys okay?" I ask.

"A few broken ribs, my body will heal soon," Buusta says, holding his side.

"I'll be okay," Rob responds. "Are you okay?"

"I'll be fine, I think." I look around at the empty area around us. "Everybody seems to have run away."

"We better get out of here," Buusta says, getting up off the lizard-man.

We clear the glass off the seats and luckily, my car still runs. Back in my apartment, there's a knock at the door. When I check the peephole, I see it's Gideon.

Will my life ever be normal again? I ponder for a moment, then let him in.

"Nice to see you again, Sam." Gideon comes in. He sees Buusta and simply gives a nod and says, "Buusta." He looks at Rob and gives him a slight nod of recognition.

"You know Buusta?" I ask.

"I know all the Chosen," Gideon replies.

"This is Gideon," I say to Rob. "Gideon, this is Rob."

"Let's get down to business," Gideon begins. "We need to destroy an earth orb in Realm Three or there will be more rifts between realms." He looks at me with a level of intensity. "Have you accepted your place as a Chosen soldier?"

"I don't know about all that, but I will help destroy that orb thingy," I respond. "I don't want more enemies like those two we just fought coming here."

"Can the guy who cast that spell on Sam's jacket cast a spell on something that I can have, so I can fight, too?" Rob asks.

"He could, but he probably wouldn't," Gideon replies. "If you're serious about helping, I can take you to a place where you can train. Don't decide now, just think about it."

"When do we leave?" I ask.

"In two days," Gideon replies. "Since you haven't accepted your place as a Chosen, I'll need to get a couple of items which are basically round-trip tickets between realms. They're hard to come by."

Gideon looks over at Rob. "Decide if you want to be trained. I'll see you all soon."

———

Rob, Buusta and I talk until it's nighttime. I learn a lot about Buusta's realm and about the Chosen. There are a maximum of five Chosen soldiers in each realm, and they can travel freely between realms. Five evil soldiers from each realm can travel between the realms, as well. In Buusta's realm, each person is a humanoid animal or at least has an animal form they can change into.

Rob stays the night. He doesn't completely trust Buusta.

———

The next day, I see myself on the news. Apparently, there was someone who was taking pictures of me during my fight with the fox-person and of me rescuing people from the burning building. The news anchor says, "We have a real-life superhero. I call her The Leather Jacket."

People in the newsroom erupt with laughter. I can tell he chose the name because in a lot of the pictures, much of my clothing was burned off yet my jacket was fine. I don't really see any humor in the name, but it doesn't bother me.

The day is mostly uneventful and a welcome reprieve with all the recent craziness. Rob decides to train so he is able to help me fight. He says, "I can be your sidekick." He quits his job, calls his parents and says he wants to travel the country for a while.

———

I'm on the news again the next day. They have multiple interviews with people who saw me fight the fox-person and others who saw me when I was fighting crime.

Gideon comes by in the afternoon, and we all get into his car. I'm kind of surprised he has one.

We drive into the country and go down dirt

roads. We stop after a while and walk into the woods. Eventually, we come upon what seems to be an abandoned building. We go into it.

Gideon looks over at Rob. "Have you decided?"

"I want to be trained," Rob replies. "I told my parents that I'm traveling the country, so I can be gone for a while."

"You'll be fine. Time is different between realms," Gideon says. "The place you're going, you can train for a year there and only a day will go by here." Gideon puts a small stone on Rob's forehead, and it disappears into his head.

"Saalem," Gideon says, and a gray portal opens up where a wall once was. "Just walk in. I'll be right behind you."

Rob walks into it, disappearing.

The portal closes. Gideon comes over to me and puts a small stone on my forehead. It disappears into my head.

"Borshes," Gideon says, and a portal opens up. Buusta goes through the portal and I'm a little nervous, but I follow after a moment. I feel like I'm being stretched. It's a little painful, but bearable. After what seems like ten minutes, I appear in a forested area.

We're standing on a surface made of some type of smooth gray stone. The stone ground forms a big circle surrounded by dense trees.

Buusta takes off the clothes I lent him. "Take off your clothes."

"What?" I exclaim.

Buusta walks to a pile of clothes at the edge of the circle. The pile consists of brown pants, black shirts and gray shoes.

Buusta hands me clothes. "If stuff from another realm leaves the portal area, it vaporizes. Fortunately, magic items and a couple other things don't. So, your jacket will be fine."

He moves to the edge of the circle and turns around, giving me privacy. I dress in the new clothes, putting on my jacket last. The garments are uncomfortable and I worry they may irritate my skin.

"My village isn't far from here," Buusta says.

We begin walking down a path between trees. They are tall and thick and smell like pine, though I can tell they're not pine trees.

We exit the forest and proceed to move at a faster pace. I'm sweating from the heat and humidity.

We get to Buusta's village. It has a bunch of yurts and teepees on the ground and bridges connecting trees up in the air.

"We'll have to find Zander," Buusta says, motioning for me to continue following him.

We walk past multiple wolf-people, who are

silent and unwelcoming, and get to a large yurt, where inside is a man who looks Asian. He is a little taller than I am in my 'guy form.' He's lean and seems like he might be muscular, but I'm not sure due to the loosely fit black robe and baggy black pants he's wearing. He has short, spiky black hair.

"Who's this?" he asks Buusta.

"This is Sam, a Chosen from Realm Seven," Buusta replies. To me, he says, "This is Zander from Realm Two."

"Nice to meet you," I say.

Zander gives me a small bow, then looks at Buusta. "We need to destroy the orb as soon as possible."

Buusta nods. "We will get ready today to move out first thing tomorrow."

Zander leaves the yurt.

Buusta takes me to his own yurt.

"The Naasdo tribe has the orb," he explains. "They are a tiger tribe. They are being used by Lucien."

Buusta introduces me to his tribe. There are about fifty of them. I'm not sure whether they don't like me or if they're just being cautious of a newcomer. The tribe has primitive weapons, spears, stone knives, throwing axes, and bows and arrows.

It's late morning when Zander comes to us. He has three swords with curved blades in sheaths —

one on his left hip, one on his right and another in his hand. They look like katanas. He gives the one he's holding to me.

"I don't know how to sword fight." I say.

"You'll learn. I'll teach you," Zander says. "It's a week's travel to get to the Naasdo."

We congregate with Buusta's tribe in what appears to be the middle point of the yurts. Everyone has their weapons and supplies for the trip. We begin the journey.

———

The first two days of the trip are long and hot. Both nights, Zander teaches me some basics of sword fighting. He has two wooden swords that we use for practice and sparring. He also tells me some things about his realm. Ninety-five percent of the people in his world speak the same language. There are five officially recognized countries, and three others that are not. The three nations that aren't accepted as sovereign are known as the triad, and he's from one of them. They are considered illegitimate due to their small size and lack of military strength.

The third night under the stars and moonlight, he says. "I want to show you something." He takes off his shirt to reveal a muscular body. He gets into a crouching stance. He then yells, "Thunderclap!" He surges forward, drawing his swords and striking the air with impressive speed. Scattered lightning surrounds him and his swords.

"I call that attack the X strike," Zander says, sheathing his swords.

I assume he calls it that because his swords criss-cross, kind of making an X during the attack.

"My clan has a rare gene. The government that controls the country I'm from in my realm injected all of my clan with a drug. It killed over half of us right away. It gave the survivors the ability to use electricity by combining our mind Ukkosen and body Salama. We call this ability Ukkosen Salama, or the technical term Ukkosen Jyrahdys."

He looks up at the sky. "A lot more of my clan died in combat soon after obtaining this ability. Using it too much can hurt our organs. Only I and four others of my clan are still alive. The other four are also Chosen. There's my cousin, Han, who uses electricity with hand-to-hand combat and sends lightning bolts at enemies. There's my cousin, Rudolf, he's an assassin. My sister, Luca. She mostly uses electricity with some ranged weapons, including bows and arrows. She needs to use them to channel and control the electricity."

Zander's demeanor then changes to one of adoration.

"And my father, Thor. He is very old, but looks

about my age. He's one of the founders of the Chosen. There are stories of him in multiple realms, but they never seem to get his appearance right."

"I'd like to visit your realm and meet your family in the future," I say, looking at the sky with him.

"I'm sure you will at some point." Zander yawns.

"Oh, I should mention, in case you didn't know. Chosen stop aging at twenty-five." Zander yawns again. "It has something to do with the brain, I think. If we're older than twenty-five when we're Chosen, we stop aging immediately."

———

He continues to train me this night and the nights following. The days are as long and hot as the beginning of our journey.

We get within eye-shot of the Naasdo tribe's base. All we can see is its large wooden walls; what's inside is a mystery. The base is wide open, surrounded by sparse vegetation. We waste no time, as most of Buusta's tribe begin shooting arrows over the wall. The gate of the fortress opens and a stream of tiger-people wielding swords emerge. Buusta's tribe shoot more and more enemies as they get closer to us. When they get close, Buusta and most of his brethren switch weapons to spears.

We begin melee fighting and quickly finish off

our assailants. About eight of Buusta's tribesmen lie dead on the battlefield. The rest of us rush into the fortress before the gates can close.

The fortress is fairly large, with wooden buildings. A giant tiger-person with a gargantuan sword stands between us and the orb.

About a dozen wolf-men charge the giant tiger-man but he slices them down with three quick sword strokes.

Zander, unfazed, charges him. Zander deflects a sword strike with one of his swords, but the collision snaps his in two, leaving a large knife's worth of the blade. He jumps up and stabs the giant in the right eye. The giant yells, punching Zander in the midsection, sending him hurtling backwards.

I spring into action, charging the giant as he charges me. He swings at me several times but I dodge each attack. He swings down with impressive force. I deflect his sword with mine as I jump to the side, barely dodging the blow that snaps my sword to the hilt. The tiger-man's sword is embedded in the ground. I jump up, punching him in his one good eye; he grabs his face and backs up.

At this, I grab his sword hilt, using all my strength to get it out of the ground, and raise the sword high. The giant squints, trying to see out his remaining eye. I can tell in this moment that I can strike him down, ending his life.

I freeze.

The giant withdraws a large knife from a holster on the back of his belt. He slashes at me. Zander, who is standing again, frowns as he takes off his shirt.

"Thunderclap!" he shouts, surging forward amid purple lightning. His attack is so fast it barely registers in my mind. With one slash, he cuts through the giant's neck, decapitating him.

Blood rains down on me as the giant's corpse falls to my feet.

Zander comes up next to me. "Good job," he says sarcastically, then immediately seems to regret it when he sees I'm in shock. "Sorry, are you all right?"

Before I'm able to respond, he spins around. His eyes go wide as he sees a man who comes out of a wooden hut with a large, long sword. The sword isn't as big as the giant's, but if he can wield it properly, it will be startling. He is in a somewhat muscular human form, a little over 6 feet tall with short brown hair. A scar stands out on his right cheek. He is intimidating.

"Doran," Zander almost whispers, obviously a little shaken.

The man grins, walks over to the orb and holds it for a moment. He gives us another grin before tossing it to Zander.

"Why aren't you trying to stop us?" Zander

exclaims with confusion. "You're one of Lucien's men."

"I have my reasons," the man says before going to one of the huts. He jumps on it, then jumps over the wall.

I help finish off the few remaining tiger-men, then we calmly deliver the orb to Buusta.

Buusta holds the orb in one hand for just a moment before smashing it with his other fist. The orb shatters.

I feel sick to my stomach. I'm not sure if this is because I ended the lives of intelligent beings or I'm covered in blood and losing adrenaline. Probably both.

A little over half of Buusta's tribe is dead. There's no celebrating; we bury the dead in solemn silence. Night seems to come slowly. We light fires and stories are spoken of the fallen.

———

The next day, as we head back, Zander continues to teach me sword fighting.

I ask him about the guy he called Doran, but he doesn't want to talk about him. I ask why the lightning in the attack that killed the giant was purple. He tells me that channeling electricity from different parts of his body causes the electricity to be different colors. Using a specific color too much hurts the whole body, but it hurts a specific organ more.

The week-long trip back seems to take a lot longer, but we eventually arrive in Buusta's village.

"I need to go back to my realm," Zander says to Buusta.

"I should head back, too," I say.

Buusta escorts us to where the portal spit us out into this realm. He and Zander turn around as I change.

"Don't you need to change, too?" I ask.

"I came here nude," Zander says, adding, "I'll keep these clothes on since a lady is present."

He says, "Suomi," and a portal opens up.

Zander approaches Buusta who kisses him tenderly. They begin kissing vigorously for a couple of moments until Zander lays his forehead on Buusta's chest. Buusta holds him gently.

"Sydameni ... Rakkaani ... Minun Alfa," says Zander right before they end their short embrace.

"What did you say?" Buusta asks.

"I just said bye and I'll see you soon," Zander replies.

The public display of affection catches me off-guard and I feel a little awkward after the initial surprise wears off.

Zander goes to the portal and says, "Stay safe,"

right before winking and jumping backwards, disappearing. The portal closes.

Buusta says, "Atlenta" and another portal opens. "That's your realm. I'm staying here. My tribe needs me."

I think for a moment, then give him a quick hug and then wave, saying, "Take care." I walk into the portal. The trip back to my realm is the same as when I left it.

I come out in the old, abandoned house I left from. Gideon is waiting for me with Rob. He looks different. He has long hair now, some of it gray. He looks older and tired. He's wearing black robes.

"Finally!" Rob yells with a smile. He comes over to me, giving me a big hug. "I've missed you so much."

I can tell he's gained a lot of muscle and lost a good deal of weight.

"I missed you, too. You look different," I smile. "I love your robes."

"Thanks. Portals don't affect them. I'm glad because I really have become emotionally attached to them. I'm probably, like, five years older," Rob responds.

Gideon, Rob and I talk for a little bit before we head back to the car. Rob tells me about his training. It sounds hellish. He trained in hand-to-hand combat and how to use a wide variety of weapons, including guns.

Rob tells me the human brain has about a thousand mental blocks that can be unblocked for a while. If unblocked, they can give you increased speed and strength, but it's dangerous and can damage the body. He says he can unblock about ninety-three.

We get to the car and something occurs to me. "How long have I been gone?"

"About a week has gone by in this realm," Gideon replies. "Time between realms is complicated and changing."

"Yeah, so Gideon and I waited in that house for about two days," Rob says, getting close to me to whisper, "Gideon's not really a conversationalist."

We drive back to my apartment, and Gideon says, "I'll be in contact," before leaving.

Rob and I stay up late talking. Apparently, with his training program he could have trained for thirteen years, but it becomes increasingly difficult, intense and dangerous. He stopped after five years. Most trainees quit shortly after arriving, and most who don't quit then stop after a year. Only a few people have made it through all thirteen years.

He crashes on my couch. The morning comes fast. Rob is already up when I wake up. We decide to go out for breakfast.

We get within walking distance of the diner and park. This area of the city is busy. There's a bit of a walk from where we park to the restaurant. The weather is nice for the most part.

Rob buys a newspaper from a gas station on the way.

We increase our walking speed to just a little slower than a jog. We're both really hungry.

"You bought a newspaper?" I ask, slightly surprised for some reason.

"I'm curious about what's going on and I'm away from my computer," he says, misinterpreting my reaction of surprise as being slightly judgmental. "You know I don't own a cellphone and if I did, it probably wouldn't be one I could check the news on."

"How much did the newspaper cost, out of curiosity?" I ask, genuinely wanting to know.

He tells me and it becomes obvious he still thinks I'm judging him. He doesn't seem to be bothered, but it's noticeable.

"You know, I think it's kind of cool you don't have a cellphone." I smile and shove him playfully. "It's classic Robert."

Rob laughs and grins. "Classic me."

———

We get to the restaurant, and it's not crowded. A cute blonde waitress who looks to be in her early twenties takes us to a booth. She seems like she finds Rob attractive; she's even a little flustered and a bit curious about the robes he's wearing.

Rob is like a brother to me as well as my best friend, but he's objectively hot now. Rob doesn't notice her attraction even though it's obvious.

We sit down and order. Rob gets eggs, bacon and sausage. I get pancakes and eggs. Rob begins moaning a little as he eats. "I haven't eaten meat since I left," he says, trying to compose himself.

As we eat, he suddenly says, "It's really nice to be around women again."

He looks around the diner at the few groups of people eating. "You're the first woman I've seen in five years," Rob adds absent-mindedly.

I find this really touching. Because he didn't even think about it; it didn't register in his mind that there was any difference between me and a woman who's not trans, and because he has no reaction that suggests he realizes that he said it without thinking. He just continues eating.

"It was a bit of a sausage fest there," he laughs while examining the sausage impaled on his fork. "God, it feels good to laugh. The place where I trained was always ridiculously serious, even by my standards."

We continue eating and Rob begins to read the newspaper.

Rob abruptly goes from calm and mellow to intense and angry. His body becomes rigid, and his facial features set in a rage. The atmosphere becomes thick with tension. He seems like he's struggling not to explode.

It's scary. I've never seen him this angry. Heck, I've never seen him more than a bit annoyed.

A couple moments go by. It seems like forever.

"Rob?" I say quietly.

He looks at me and for a split second I see something in his eyes that shakes me to my core. This happens for only a split second as his brain snaps out of its state of mind at the sight of me.

He puts one of his hands over his face for a moment. "Sorry," he mumbles.

"Are you okay?" I ask.

"I'll be fine," he says, visibly sad.

"What is it?" I lean forward, putting my hand on his shoulder.

He hands me the paper.

An article says that in parts of my country, parents of kids who are trans are being investigated for abuse if the kids receive medical care related to being trans. The families are being forced to move to other parts of the country or risk losing their kids. It also mentions that if teachers find out a student is gay or trans, they are legally required to tell the parents.

I sit still for a moment, absorbing the information, then say the first thing that comes to my mind. "Teachers being forced to out kids is going to cause a lot of child abuse."

I don't say this part, but I think, *Even putting that aside, kids do deserve some privacy. Depending on the parents, them finding out could cause physical, sexual, emotional, physiological abuse.*

I assume I look confused and disturbed.

"They want you dead."

Rob starts talking to me like ... It's hard to describe. The way he starts talking to me is kind of like when a close friend is explaining to another friend that they're in a really abusive relationship.

"They want trans people dead. They want trans adults dead. And they want the kids who are trans to be dead. Or at least not to exist, which is a distinction without a difference."

"But ..." I begin feeling numb and a little lightheaded.

"They want you dead. There are no levels to it, no complexity. They just want you dead."

———

We finish eating and go back to my place. After listening to music and talking for a while, the mood returns to normal, or close to normal.

"I need to tell my parents that I'm not going to travel the country," Rob says. "I'm just going to tell them I went on a quick road trip for a week."

He changes out of his robes in preparation.

"Bye, I'll see you soon," Rob says. We hug.

"You might want to get a haircut or you'll confuse your parents," I say with a smile.

"Yeah, I'm glad I kept my clothes. The robes might have weirded them out a bit, too. Bye," Rob says before leaving.

———

The rest of the day, I start to get really depressed. I see on the news that most places have made it illegal for people who are trans to use the restroom they want. A few places have made it so we can't use either restroom, justifying it with the weird excuse of increased assaults on us. They talk about how some places are legally forcing teachers to out kids to the community. I see most places have banned people under eighteen from transitioning or are trying to. And law makers are raising the age higher and higher, making it so adults can't transition, either. I'm overwhelmed and fall into a deeper depression.

———

A week goes by, and Rob and I make a plan. I realize it's extra-dangerous to fight crime by myself, so we decide to protect the city together.

Rob and I begin fighting crime frequently, and we work well together. Similar to when I fought by myself, we ignore things that are illegal yet victimless. Rob starts to show me how to fight better. People start taking pictures and sometimes videos of us. We go viral on social media. They call me "The Leather Jacket," probably because of the joke that news anchor made when a lot of my clothes were burned off and my jacket was fine. They call Rob "Monk" because his robes look like he could be from a monastery. When we go out at night, I bring a wooden katana and a regular katana; Rob wears his robes and brings a bow staff, a long sword and a gun.

"Even the best martial artists should carry a gun in certain situations," he says. "Even with my training, a bullet could still take me out easily."

This goes on for a few months. Gideon doesn't contact us.

———

On a random night, Rob and I are patrolling the city like we usually do when we see several demonic figures come out from the shadows. They are the average height of a man, with gray skin and tiny horns. They attack us, and we slice through them with our swords.

"What the hell?" I say right before a larger group of them comes down the block.

Rob and I slice through demon after demon. We make a good team. Rob gets hit by one of their claws that cuts through his robes and goes across his chest. The demons start to dwindle, then the air gets tense. A 7-foot-tall scaly demon appears from seemingly nowhere with more of his minions. He charges me, and I slash at him as he closes in on me. He grabs my blade and squeezes, shattering it. He then kicks me in the chest, sending me sprawling down the road.

Rob shoots the new demon, using all the bullets in his revolver. The demon punches Rob with great intensity, knocking him down to one knee.

The demon continues towards me, leaving Rob to the remainder of his subordinates.

He charges me again, punching at me as he gets close. I block but it hurts badly. I draw my wooden sword, which is quickly snapped in two by the demon's kick. We continue fighting. I keep on dodging most of his attacks. I'm faster, but he's stronger.

After a while, I land several strikes at his ribs, seemingly hurting him, but then I mess up, allowing him to hit me in the head. I fall to the ground, then get on my hands and knees. He kicks me in the side, sending me spinning into the air. I land on my back.

I see someone jumping from a three-story building. He's semi-muscular and wearing a gray leather jacket and gray pants. He has headphones around his neck and a black bandanna on his head. He has a long sword strapped to his back. As he falls, he shoots the demon with two long-barreled handguns. He looks like a badass.

The demon is obviously hurt and moving slowly. The newcomer unsheathes the sword on his back. He slices through the fazed demon, which quickly turns into reddish salt.

The new fighter comes over to me, helping me up. I see his face and take a stunned step back, looking him up and down. I'm in shock.

"Thomas?"

SEVEN

"Thomas, is that you?" I ask.

"Yeah. Hey, Sam." We rush into each other's embrace.

"How?" I ask, full of emotions.

Suddenly, my attention shifts.

"Rob!"

Thomas and I rush to where I last saw Rob. He's still there, but now surrounded by corpses of demons that slowly turn to reddish salt. He looks hurt.

"Are you okay?" I catch Rob as he begins to fall.

"I'll be fine," Rob replies. He looks over at Thomas and doesn't recognize him. "Who's that?"

"That's Thomas," I reply. "Let's go back to my place."

We get to my apartment without anything relevant happening and, surprisingly enough, without talking very much. I'm still processing everything. When we're safe in my apartment, I help get Rob to the couch and turn to Thomas.

"How?"

"I was revived by Rime, the man who cast the spell on that jacket. So, it does that to you," Thomas blushes.

Something occurs to me.

"How did you recognize me?"

"I was told what you look like in that form," Thomas replies.

The shock begins to wear off, and I try to hold back tears.

"I really missed you," I sob, hugging him.

"I missed you, too."

He kisses me tenderly.

Thomas, Rob and I talk for a few hours. Among other things, Thomas tells us about his training and that he wasn't allowed to come see me until now. He shows me his headphones.

"As you know, I've always had extra sensitivity. Now that's intensified and enhanced. I have these headphones for if I'm overwhelmed by them. I also have this bandanna to cover my eyes if I need to. I can fight with either or even both, but the majority of the time I don't need them."

Thomas and I go to bed. I fall asleep in his arms.

The morning comes quickly. When I wake up, he's stroking my hair, and the sun beating down on us from the window creates a pleasant, warm feeling. I smile and look in his eyes, kissing him. He kisses me back. He puts one of his arms around my lower back and pushes my body up tightly against his. We open our mouths and French kiss, deeply.

I sigh, feeling peace and a joy beyond anything I could ever have imagined.

EIGHT

THOMAS, Rob and I start fighting crime together. We crack down hard and let the gangs and their leaders know that in order to have us ease up, they have to implement my plan — where each of the gangs sends out one person each month to fistfight to resolve issues. We are successful.

People start calling Thomas, "Thomas," because for some reason he told someone his name.

I think long and hard. I decide to quit school because of how crazy and uncertain my life is, and I decide to be one of the Chosen.

We fight crime regularly, similar to how Rob and I did, just safer now because we have Thomas backing us up. We continue our work as vigilantes until one day there's a knock at my door. It's Gideon. I let him into my apartment.

"Call your friend and have him come here," he says.

Thomas is by my side.

"Hello to you, too," he says, with a touch of sarcasm.

I call Rob, who says he's coming over.

I tell Gideon I accept my position as one of the Chosen.

"You have been chosen to be one of this realm's warriors," Gideon says to Rob when he enters my apartment.

"Bitchin'," Rob exclaims excitedly.

Gideon looks at us.

"I should mention that being resurrected from the dead is very rare and even when it's possible you only get one mulligan."

"What?" I ask, confused.

"Oh, I forgot. You don't have that in this realm," Gideon says. "If you die and everything happens perfectly and you get revived, that can only happen once. You can only be resurrected once."

We plan to leave for the realm transporter.

"Maybe John and Travis would want to train like I did," Rob says. "We should ask them to come over."

"Maybe they can be Chosen, too," I say as the thought occurs to me.

Gideon shakes his head.

"There are already two others who have been

chosen from this realm, so with you three that's five. But your friends can train if they want to."

"Do we get to meet the other Chosen from this realm?" I ask.

"They're currently on missions in other realms. Though you'll meet them sooner or later," Gideon says. "I have missions for you. I'll be here in two days to take us to the portal. I will get two of those stones like last time, in case your friends wish to train."

Gideon leaves.

John and Travis come over. Rob has already told them everything that is going on. As they sit on my couch, Rob says, "Would you like to train to fight and help Sam and me? There's a place you can train for a year while only a day goes by here."

"That sounds great. Sign me up," Travis responds excitedly.

"I can't," John replies.

"Why not?" Travis lies back on the couch, disappointed.

"You remember in middle school when I was gone for like a month on a family vacation?" John asks, looking sad.

"Vaguely." Travis leans forward.

"I remember that," Rob says, looking concerned.

"I was in a psychiatric hospital. My brain has a chemical imbalance. I'm bipolar. I need to take medication every day, and I get shots once every three months."

John looks embarrassed.

"Oh, sorry man. We didn't know," Rob says.

John sighs.

"People look at you differently when they know you have a mental illness. I'm completely fine on medication, but without it my brain wouldn't work properly."

"We don't see you any differently now." I put a hand on his shoulder.

"I can still train in this realm." John looks determined. "I'll be there for all of you."

The next two days are uneventful. We mentally prepare to go on an unknown mission.

———

Gideon shows up at my apartment. Thomas, Rob, Travis and I are ready.

The ride to the portal is uneventful and slightly cramped with five of us in the small vehicle.

"You are going to Salaam," Gideon says, looking at Travis. He turns to Thomas, Rob and me. "You three are splitting up."

"Bullshit. I'm not leaving Sam," Thomas says, a little too aggressively.

"Same here," Rob adds.

It takes a while, but Gideon convinces us to go along with his plan.

He puts a stone on Travis' forehead, and it disappears into his head.

"Salaam," Gideon says. "I'll see you on the other side in a moment."

The portal opens, and Travis goes through.

Gideon turns to me.

"You're next. You'll meet up with Zander on the other side." He turns back towards the portal. "Dartis."

The portal opens and as I'm about to go through, I hear Thomas say, "If anything happens to her, I'm holding you accountable."

I go through the portal, and the trip to Dartis is similar to the back-and-forth trips to Borshes. I think of Thomas and my friends and their safety.

I pop out into a wide clearing. Large circles of stones surround me. Outside the stone circles are lush green meadows. The sun is beginning to set. Close by are three figures who startle me. I quickly calm down after recognizing one of them as Zander.

Standing next to Zander is a 4-foot humanoid-rodent, slender with surprisingly big ears. She has brownish eyes, a cute, small nose and whiskers.

Next to them is a tall muscular woman with black hair who looks formidable. She'd be intimidating if not for her calm expression and kind smile.

"Hello, Sam, it's nice seeing you again," Zander says. He gestures toward the large woman. "This is Sara, a Chosen from this realm." He then gestures towards the other. "And this is Baeu, a Chosen from Buusta's realm and a member of a Jerboa tribe."

"This is Sam," Zander says to the two of them.

"Hi," Baeu says, with a nod.

"Nice to meet you," Sara adds.

Zander walks over to a pile of clothes that are similar to those he's wearing. He hands some to me. "These can go in and out of portal areas a few times before disintegrating."

He looks down at the two katanas tied to his hip, then to a third he's holding. He smiles, handing me the katana in his hand.

"This is a lower-quality version of mine. Portals won't affect it. I can't believe I got my hands on Helsinki blades."

Zander goes back to the other two and turns to face away from me. Baeu and Sara follow his lead, turning around.

I change clothes, putting my original clothing by the edge of the circle, along with the gun Thomas gave me, the sword I came with and my cellphone.

"I'm done," I say.

They turn around.

"Could someone come here and take my stuff?" I ask.

"People who are not Chosen can't enter portal areas without a Chosen to accompany them. Your stuff will be fine," Zander says. "Most non-Chosen can't even see the portal area anyway."

We head towards the setting sun and come upon a little campsite with four tents. Baeu starts a fire with what looks like flint and steel. We all sit by the fire and eat sausages and fried potatoes.

"What did Gideon tell you about the Chosen and the realms?" Zander asks before taking another bite of sausage.

I think for a moment before responding.

"He told me there are twelve realms that make up existence and five Chosen from each realm. I'm from the Seventh Realm. There's a person named Lucien who is trying to take over the realms, and he is the right-hand man of the most evil being imaginable. It's our job to stop him. That's about it."

Zander nods.

"He should have told you more. The realms and everything were created by a god. Before that god died, it had two offspring — fraternal twins, one male and one female. The female has a propensity for law and order and took up the mantle of the Maiden. The male has a propensity for chaos and took up the mantle of the Demon."

Zander cracks his neck, lays down on one arm and continues.

"Gideon's a commander. Our leader is a man named Rime, the right-hand man of the Maiden, who is at war with the Demon. The Maiden is not pure good, but far better than the Demon. If one is to control the realms, I choose the Maiden."

Zander sighs.

"Sorry. I know this is a lot of information. There is a third, far weaker offspring of the creator god — Suriel, the god of neutrality, who fights for a balance between law and chaos. She is confined to this realm, and she created an order called the Numbers. Lucien was one of them before he turned into a soldier of chaos, the Demon's right-hand man."

I close my eyes and rub my forehead, soaking in the information.

"So, what's our mission?" I ask, ready to get to the point.

"The first thing we need to do is destroy another orb," Zander says. "After we destroy the orb, we'll go to a group I lead called Dragons of the Dawn. Now, I think it's time for bed," Zander says with a yawn. "We have an early start tomorrow."

We travel for two days, then reach our destination.

NINE

THE AIR IS heavy with humidity as the summer sun beats down. Off in the distance, the clamor of hooves sounding against uneven cobblestone gradually becomes apparent. Two dozen feet off the ground, Zander, Baeu, Sara and I lie in wait close to the road, perched on one of the outstretched limbs of a giant, old, sturdy oak tree, one of many.

I breathe heavily because of the heat, but also due to nervousness about the task at hand. We are laser-focused and ready. A cool breeze blows quickly, slightly alleviating our discomfort. I emit an unintentional, small yet audible grunt when the breeze subsides, which is quickly silenced by Zander.

Entering our line of sight are the sources of the strengthening clamor — a horse-drawn caravan consisting of three wagons, each drawn by two horses. Each pair of horses is directed by a civilian escorted by two guards in dull full-plate armor behind a lead wagon escorted by a man covered from head to toe in ornate glistening armor.

Zander glances at Baeu, then towards Sara and me. We quickly look in each other's directions then silently drop to the ground and start off towards the caravan, still attempting to keep hidden in the tree canopy.

As the caravan draws near, Zander readies himself for the initial assault. He retrieves a circular object from his pocket and surveys the oncoming force. He takes aim, steadies himself and throws the object. It flies true and strikes the lip of the middle wagon. We shield our faces and cover our ears.

One moment later the object erupts in an extremely bright flash and the sound of thunder cracking.

The man leading the horses in the middle wagon convulses violently, then dives headfirst into the ground. The moment the civilian strikes the ground, horses panic.

The middle wagon's horses buck, loosening their harnesses and stampeding into the forest, leaving the wagon behind. The rear wagon's harnesses remain intact, with fleeing horses carrying the wagon and driver along with them into the forest.

The front wagon's horses surge forward and trample the leading man in ornate armor, continuing with the wagon into the forest.

The remaining four soldiers rush towards their fallen captain, dazed from the explosion. Baeu and Sara jump out of the forest throwing knives that find their marks, killing two.

The others rush forward as Zander and I meet them, swords in hand. Zander blocks two quick sword strikes, then plunges his blade through one man's chest. I block an attack, then slice through the other soldier's legs. He gasps in surprise and falls to the ground. His shock is overpowered by pain, and he begins screaming. I lop off his head.

I feel a heaviness from the life I took. It feels similar to the feeling I had after killing the fox-woman and after the battle in Buusta's realm.

"You're getting better," Zander says looking at me. He points to the wagon now in front of us. "This is the one."

Zander and I begin searching. The wagon is lined with brown wooden crates that nearly touch the canvas roof.

We begin opening crates at an alarming rate, almost as if we are worried about being caught. Most contain copper or silver coins. Just as we begin to worry that we might have picked the wrong wagon, Zander finds it — a black orb. He repeatedly smashes it with the hilt of his sword until it falls apart and turns to dust.

We leave the wagon and meet up with Baeu and Sara just as a figure leaps out of the forest with a determined demeanor.

"Gideon?" Zander exclaims.

Gideon catches his breath.

"Thomas and your friend have been kidnapped."

Gideon repeats himself.

"Thomas and your friend have been kidnapped."

I start having trouble breathing. The two people I care for most are in danger. My chest hurts and the world around me seems to spin. I quickly stop myself from blaming myself for not being there to regain my composure.

Gideon moves towards the general direction of the portal.

"We must go to Hades, the ninth Realm."

Zander, Gideon and I leave immediately for the long journey out of this realm.

———

We arrive exhausted, sweaty and smelly. We go through the realm portal after Zander proclaims, "Hades."

The first thing that hits me on the other side is the humid atmosphere. The second is the smell of what can best be described as rotten eggs.

"Do we know who kidnapped Thomas and Rob?" I ask, surprised I haven't asked that before. It's been hard processing the fact that they could be hurt, if not worse.

"I'm not completely sure," Gideon replies. "I don't know everything. I do know where they're being held. It's a stronghold of Lucien's, so they're probably being held by one of his generals."

"Wait, is Travis okay?" I ask.

"He was taken to his home by a Chosen from your realm. He quit within two weeks of training, so it was like no time passed in your realm for him. Don't be disappointed in him. Most people can't make it through a couple of days training there, let alone a full year," Gideon replies to my surprised look "Quick, there's no time to lose."

We journey at a fast, steady yet sustainable speed for what feels like an eternity but is likely less than a couple of hours. I'm impressed Gideon is seemingly unaffected by the heat and humidity. We walk for what seems like a mile more with Gideon continuing to lead the way. We reach our destination: a large castle on a small hill. We enter and find the inside surprisingly cool. On the door closing, the odor of rotten eggs is replaced with the smell of burning leaves.

"They should be right this way."

Gideon leads us through room after room, then down a winding staircase. I'm perturbed by the lack of opposition and the seemingly unnatural silence.

Finally, we enter a large room with corpses littering the floor. There's a stage opposite the door. On said stage are Thomas and Rob, tied up and gagged.

Zander and I start running to them. As we get about three dozen feet from them, we start to hear Gideon clapping behind us.

"Sixteen Chosen lie at your feet. You four are the last Chosen I needed to fall into my trap. Now that I have captured twenty, Lucien will make me a general." Gideon stops clapping. "Lucien should be ruler of the realms, not the Maiden and not the Demon." He sighs contentedly. "First things first, we must get rid of all the Maiden's Chosen, then the Demon's Chosen, who refuse to align with Lucien. The next step is to get rid of you four."

Gideon snaps his fingers and the corpses rise, brandishing weapons. There are sixteen of them. Their eyes glow red.

Zander takes off his shirt, tossing it to the side. "They look tough. I might need to use the Ukkonen Salama multiple times."

As we fight the corpses, I notice a tall, red demon standing by Thomas and Rob.

Zander and I take out several corpses with great difficulty.

Suddenly something hits me hard. I go tumbling into a wall. I realize it is the demon. He slowly comes up to me as I get up. I slash at him with my sword, but he grabs my blade. There is a high-pitched noise and my sword shatters.

The demon and I punch and kick each other for a while. I change tactics, dodging his blows and hitting him with small jabs. He hits me with a powerful punch, and I start to get hit by every one of his attacks. I get more and more bloody and bruised. It becomes harder and harder to breathe, and my sight becomes blurry.

The demon grabs and throws me on the podium next to Thomas and Rob. He leaps onto the stage. He takes off my jacket and I transform. He throws my jacket far to the side.

I can tell the demon is hurt.

If only I still had my jacket, I might be able to stop him, I think to myself.

The demon ungags his captives. "Any last words," he asks in a deep voice, "before I kill you all?"

Rob looks like he's about to cry. "You're my best

friend," he says to me before his voice chokes with sobs.

Thomas looks at me tenderly.

"I love you. I'm sorry it has to end like this." He gives me a beautiful smile. "I just want you to know. I know you feel more comfortable transformed, but as far as I'm concerned you are always my Sam, and you're sexy in any form. To me, you never needed the jacket."

I glance over at Zander, and all hopes of him saving us vanishes. I hear "Thunderclap!" multiple times as he takes down one undead after another, using many-hued electrical attacks. He's making progress, but not fast enough.

The demon moves toward Thomas, his hands becoming claws.

The last thing Thomas said replays over and over in my mind. "You never needed the jacket."

I jump to my feet as the demon gets to Thomas. He swings his clawed hand down at my boyfriend.

I lunge at my enemy, transforming without the jacket.

"Thunderclap!" I yell, mirroring a shout from Zander in the distance. Scattered electricity surrounds my body as I punch the side of the demon's forehead. He drops to one knee for a moment, his head held low.

"Zander!" I yell. He tosses me one of his swords.

I catch it and with one motion slice through the demon's neck.

The demon's head drops, severed from the rest of his body. A moment later the body drops to the ground, blood spraying from its neck.

I turn to see Gideon. His expression is one of shock. He quickly turns and exits the room. I contemplate chasing him but decide to untie Thomas and Rob instead.

Zander, who just felled the last corpse, comes up next to us. He spits a bit of blood in the opposite direction.

"That bastard!" Zander yells as he puts his shirt back on. "I never would have expected that Gideon would betray us."

I go get my jacket and put it on. Nothing happens since I'm already transformed.

The four of us converse for a little bit then leave the castle together.

As we head towards the portal to the realms, Zander keeps looking at me weirdly.

"What?" I ask, wanting him to stop.

"How the hell did you do that?" he asks, with a mixture of confusion, awe and, oddly enough, anger.

"I don't know. I guess I don't need the jacket to transform anymore," I say, still processing everything that happened in the fight.

"Not that. How did you use electrical power in an attack?" Zander asks.

"I guess the magic word just worked for me," I respond, feeling a little uncomfortable for some reason.

"It's not a magic word! Like I said before: It's biology, genetics, DNA. Thunderclap is my last name," he says, looking bewildered.

"You say your last name before you do your electrical attacks?" I respond.

"Yes," Zander sighs. "Sorry, I had to do a lot of training to even create a small amount of electricity and it took most of my life to master Ukkosen Jyrahdys. I'm not upset with *you* ..." His voice trails off for a moment before he asks, "Can you do it again?"

"I can try."

I start attacking the empty space in front of me, trying to produce electricity. It doesn't work. I start yelling "Thunderclap!" while attacking, but nothing happens.

"Oh!" I take off my jacket and try. Still nothing.

"How important is it for me to take off my shirt? When it worked, I was still wearing one."

Zander looks confused.

"Having clothing on or not doesn't affect anything."

"Then why do you take off your shirt before you do electrical attacks?"

I stop trying to use energy attacks.

"Why wouldn't I take off my shirt before doing energy attacks?" Zander responds as if I asked a ridiculous question.

We don't see Gideon or anyone else during the rest of our short journey.

Zander goes back to his realm, and Thomas, Rob and I go back to ours.

EPILOGUE

THE RUN-DOWN old house looks about the same. The sky is cloudy and it seems to be afternoon. We walk back to where Gideon parked his car; it's still there.

I get in the driver's seat.

"Shotgun," Thomas says before getting into the seat next to mine. Rob gets in the backseat.

I turn the key, but the car doesn't start. I pop the hood and Thomas checks to find the battery is dead, saying the obvious, "Yeah, the battery is dead."

Rob comes up next to Thomas.

"Shit, the engine and battery are rusty."

I join them looking at the engine.

"I'll call for a taxi," I say, doing just that.

It's dark by the time the taxi pulls up next to us. It's cold and I'm thankful for my jacket. Thomas and I get in the back. Rob sits in front.

The driver is a white guy who looks to be in his twenties. The taxi smells like burgers, like he just had fast food.

"Where are you headed?" he asks.

I tell him my address and we head in that direction.

The driver turns on the radio. There's a guy talking about degeneracy, and he says that things have never been better, that society is reaching some sort of utopia. He also almost simultaneously suggests things are really terrible. It's very weird.

The driver changes the station to classical music.

————

We get to my apartment; the time is early morning. I feel sore from being in the cramped car all night. It seems like the sun will be coming up soon.

I get to my apartment door and am unable to get in. The key doesn't work. I call the super of the apartment complex and get the answering machine. I leave a message telling him I can't get into my apartment.

We look at each other and leave the building. I think of Travis; I was told he is safe, but I'm still concerned. The sun is rising. I know I'll probably wake him up, but I call him anyway.

It rings for a while, then probably just before it goes to voice mail he picks up.

"Hello?" I hear his tired voice and assume I did in fact wake him.

"Travis, this is Sam. Sorry," I say, being cut off.

"Sam?" Travis yells.

"Yeah, are you okay?" I ask.

"Am I okay?" Travis continues to yell. "Are you okay?"

"Yeah," I say, starting to feel uneasy. "Are you okay?"

"I'm fine." Travis begins calming down. "Where have you been?"

"I've been in another realm, you know that," I say, feeling more uneasy.

"Wait! Are Rob and Thomas okay?" Travis exclaims.

"They're fine, they're with me."

Rob's eyes go wide for a moment and he looks at me with consternation. "Hand me your phone."

I hand him my phone without saying anything.

Rob puts the phone on speaker, making me wonder why he didn't just ask me to do that.

"Travis, what's going on?"

Travis sounds perplexed.

"You've all been gone for a while. I was starting to fear the worst."

His voice goes from baffled to determined.

"We need to meet up, we need to talk about some things."

"I sold my car and Rob got a ride to my place before Gideon took us to the portal," I reply.

Travis sighs.

"Where are you right now?"

"We're at my apartment," I say.

"I'll pick you up," Travis says before abruptly hanging up.

We wait about an hour, and I get a call from my landlord.

"What do you want?" he asks, sounding annoyed.

"I'm locked out of my apartment," I say.

"You stopped paying your rent, so I evicted you," he says angrily. "Don't call me again unless it's to give me the money you owe me." With that, he hangs up.

"I'm glad I had my phone on auto-pay or I wouldn't have been able to call the taxi and Travis," I say to myself.

We wait for several hours. I get a little worried because I know where Travis lives, and he should be here already.

More time passes. Just as I'm about to call Travis again, he arrives. It's late afternoon by now. He seems tense.

"Get in."

He's driving an old blue pickup truck. Rob gets in and moves up next to Travis. I can tell it's a tight fit so I try to transform because my 'guy body' is smaller. I can't do it. I take off my jacket and still don't transform.

"What's the gender on your driver's license?" Travis asks, looking at me with fear etched on his face.

"It says male. I haven't changed it yet; it even has my dead name on it," I respond. "Why?"

"Fuck!" Travis exclaims, hitting his truck's steering wheel. "You need to transform."

I repeatedly try until I get lightheaded and a little dizzy.

"I can't for some reason."

"Okay, just get in." Travis calms himself. "Your driver's license wouldn't have worked anyway. You basically need a specific identification card here. Hopefully we're not stopped by the cops, or ..."

Thomas gets in and I sit on his lap, hunched over.

Travis begins driving.

"We're going to John's place." He looks around and seems paranoid. "Give me your driver's license."

I give him my license, and he throws it out the window.

"You're safer without it. I'll explain everything when we get to John's house."

———

John's waiting outside for us with two women. He looks about the same except he seems to have embraced baldness by buzzing his remaining hair.

John rushes over to us, hugging first me tightly, then Rob. He gets to Thomas but hesitates for a moment, not sure if it'd be weird hugging him because they don't know each other that well. He hugs Thomas anyway.

Travis gestures to the woman with freckles.

"This is my girlfriend, Nora."

John gestures to the other lady.

"This is Kulta, my girlfriend," he says happily. He gestures towards Thomas, Rob and me. "This is Sam, Rob and Thomas."

We all exchange greetings.

"We need to talk," Travis says in a serious tone.

John's happy demeanor changes to match Travis'. We all go into John's house. The happy memories of John and I hanging out here seem distant. We sit in his living room; the atmosphere is tense and foreboding.

"A lot of stuff has happened since you left," John begins grimly.

"What's going on?" I shift uncomfortably in my seat.

Travis and John look at each other for a moment,

then John begins, "Things have become seriously fucked since you left."

John thinks for a moment. "The government made transitioning in general illegal for everyone." He sighs. "They've made it so that teachers and federal employees are forced to use pronouns assigned at birth and the name that's on their birth certificate."

He stops for a moment, as if the story is painful to tell.

"They banned more and more books from schools and libraries, then removed people's ability to buy them. Now there's an approved book list and all other books are banned. They made it so that all teachers everywhere had to out LGBTQ students to parents, and now that's evolved to teachers having to out students to their parents and their community."

John stops talking. He gets a little emotional and looks like he's holding back tears.

Travis looks sad and tired.

"They made segregated classrooms, removing LGBTQ kids and college students from the general population. The state frequently kidnaps kids." Travis puts one of his hands over his face. "They created lists of people in the LGBTQ community and created a sort of registry; neighbors will out other neighbors. Marriage is illegal except for straight, cisgendered couples of the same race. Most hate crimes are effectively legal now. They've enacted forced sterilization."

Travis takes his hand off his face and his sad and tired demeanor turns to anger. "The politicians took away stuff that helped regular people and created a truly horrible economy, then blamed the suffering they caused on LGBTQ people."

His anger turns into a simmering rage.

"The far right continues their constant dehumanizing and demonization propaganda of the queer community. They make it sound like the LGBTQ community is dangerous and powerful, and they claim they're creating a utopian vision of society by that exclusion."

"How could this happen?" I ask, feeling a bit frantic. "Why didn't anyone stop this?"

Travis still looks angry, but it seems like the emotion is accompanied by embarrassment.

"Most people didn't see it coming or didn't believe something like this could happen. Also, the opposition to this fascism ... We were disorganized and had a lot of infighting over stupid shit."

Travis calms down.

"The most insidious thing is there are a bunch of laws now that are super broad and vague to the point where people are breaking them all the time, but they are being selectively enforced in order to arrest people who are in the LGBTQ community.

They started by effectively criminalizing being trans, then the rest of the community, then allies and people who are opposed to the current regime."

Travis seems to stare into nothingness.

"Now people are disappearing. I think they're being taken to different 'containment camps.' We heard about them shortly before the news media and the Internet became heavily censored."

The feeling of dread fills the room. Thomas looks at me with a determined look.

"Can I use your cellphone?"

"Yeah," I say softly, feeling numb.

Thomas dials as he leaves the house. After what feels like about twenty minutes without much conversation, Thomas comes back inside and sits next to me again.

"I called Rime." He looks at John and Travis. "He's the man who rose me from the grave and made Sam's jacket magical. He should be here shortly."

I'm not ashamed to admit I'm scared. I look at Thomas.

"Hold me."

He wraps his arms around me. I feel safe being held against his chest and my fears seems to ease.

I fall asleep to the rhythm of his heartbeat.

I wake up in my original body two hours later. I'm in my jacket. I'm confused for a minute. I try focusing and will myself to transform. It works. I look up at Thomas.

"Looks like I'm transforming myself now, not the jacket."

We hear a knock at the door. I get off Thomas; he and John get up and check to see who it is.

"It's Rime," Thomas exclaims as John lets him in.

Rime is wearing his black trench coat and carrying a bag. He puts his right hand on Thomas' head for a moment.

Rime looks at all of us.

"So, you're all mostly caught up on what's going on here." He looks at Thomas, Rob and me. "Lucien has somehow created an energy that's a combination of the Demon's chaos energy, the Maiden's energy and Suriel's neutral energy. He has twisted and perverted them into something that is pure evil."

Rime sits at the kitchen table and seems to stare off into nothingness for a long moment.

"Rime ..." Thomas says softly.

Rime composes himself.

"The energy has invaded several realms, including this one. There are force fields around the death camps using this energy. We won't be able to get through them and rescue those inside unless we work together."

"So, what do we do?" Rob replies.

We start to make plans. Rime pulls me aside.

"Realm Eight is very similar to your realm. They're dealing with similar things; they just haven't gotten to this point yet."

He puts his hand on my head. A lot of knowledge about *your* realm — the realm of the person reading this book right now — rushes through my mind, being cemented into my brain.

He removes his hand and says, "I need you to write your story and warn people there. I'm not sure if it'll work or if it does, how much good it will do."

"Is there a way we can go back in time and change things?" I ask.

"No." Rime looks at me like I just said the most ridiculous thing ever. "Times between realms move at different speeds relative to each other, and the speeds can change, but time always moves forward. There's no changing the past. Ever."

He gets up and says he'll be back in a week.

———

Rob comes up next to me as I begin writing.

"What are you doing?"

"I'm writing a warning to the Eighth Realm," I respond.

I tell Rob what's going on in your realm, and

how it mimics some of the stuff that's happened in ours.

"I hope this does something," I say, feeling a mixture of emotions. "You know what they say, the pen is mightier than the sword."

"It is, as long as you've got people with swords backing you up," Rob replies.

I start sobbing.

"Whoa, are you okay?" Rob exclaims, surprised.

"Rob, what am I supposed to do? I'm just a chick in a jacket," I say, trying to compose myself.

Rob puts his arm around me.

"We do what we can. It's not just you in this fight. We fight together."

"I just wanted to be a regular superhero," I say, calmly wiping away tears. "Fight criminals and have fantasy adventures. I didn't want to deal with this level of darkness."

"We do what we gotta do," Rob begins. "We roll with the punches and play through the pain. We're forced to confront everything that going on, that's our only option."

———

I spend the next few days writing my story so far.

I spend the rest of the week editing it and trying to figure out how to end this book.

So ... how *do* I end this book?

To those who are trans, to everyone in the LGBTQ+ community and allies, to your realm's opposition to fascism and hate — yes, you're in danger, but remember:

- With all of the bad in the world, do not forget there's goodness.
- With all of the aggression, do not forget there's gentleness.
- With all the indifference, do not forget there's kindness.
- With all the disdain and malice, do not forget there is compassion.
- With all the hate, do not forget there's love.
- The good is more prevalent than the bad.
- Don't let darkness blind you from the light.
- Don't lose hope.

Awareness of evil accompanied by indifference is worthless.

(I'm including myself in this)

Now we put away petty differences.

Now we unite.

Now we fight.

If breath fills my lungs, if my heart still beats
If I'm still alive, I will write you again.
Until then,

Stay safe,
Samantha The Leather Jacket

ADVICE ROB WANTED ME TO ADD

1. Keep your passport up to date.
2. Have a backup plan.
3. Save money if you can.
4. Get involved with the LGBTQ+ community online and/or off and make some friends to help you on your journey through life.

ACKNOWLEDGMENTS

SPECIAL THANKS TO:

Betty Martinez, who did the beautiful cover art and styled the interior.

Donald Weise, who was my editor.

Cindy Dashnaw Jackson, who did the final copy-editing.

My close friend Lucas for reading and giving feedback throughout the whole process.

My Aunt M. and my friend Roberto for reading one of the drafts and giving feedback.

Ian Kochinski, for making me understand the situation we're in. Rob quoted him when he said, "They want you dead. There's no levels to it, no complexity. They just want you dead." Rob's advice at the end of the book came from Ian.

ABOUT THE AUTHOR

Chris Pelz is a self-proclaimed nerdy geek with an overactive imagination and a love for writing.

"A Call to Troll Action"

If people started responding dismissively to TERF and Fascist hate by sending them a link to buy my book, that would be hilarious.

YOU CAN FIND ME AT:

Twitter- ChrisPelz @ChrisPelzAuthor
Facebook Author Page-
facebook.com/ChrisPelzAuthor

www.ingramcontent.com/pod-product-compliance
Lightning Source LLC
Chambersburg PA
CBHW060937120626
46557CB00003B/1043